GRINGO

When Brogan McNally, saddletramp, arrives at the small Mexican town of Santa Cruz, he becomes involved with a local bandit chief, Pablo Hemenez. When Brogan is captured by the Mexican army, the only way to gain his freedom is to turn Hemenez in. A bloody battle ensues, and once Brogan is free he decides to head north. But with the whistle of lead about his head he must face an agonizing choice of life or death.

Books by L. D. Tetlow
in the Linford Western Library:

BROGAN:
TO EARN A DOLLAR
THIRTEEN DAYS
BROGAN AND THE JUDGE KILLER

L. D. TETLOW

GRINGO

Complete and Unabridged

LINFORD
Leicester

First published in Great Britain in 1996 by
Robert Hale Limited
London

First Linford Edition
published 1997
by arrangement with
Robert Hale Limited
London

British Library CIP Data

Tetlow, L. D.
 Gringo.—Large print ed.—
 Linford western library
 1. Western stories
 2. Large type books
 I. Title
 823.9′14 [F]

ISBN 0–7089–5093–0

Published by
F. A. Thorpe (Publishing) Ltd.
Anstey, Leicestershire

Set by Words & Graphics Ltd.
Anstey, Leicestershire
Printed and bound in Great Britain by
T. J. International Ltd., Padstow, Cornwall

This book is printed on acid-free paper

1

EVEN by Mexican standards, the town was very quiet, the only indication of human habitation being a shawl-clad woman dragging a young child into the single-storey adobe which was apparently home. Brogan McNally was well aware that Mexicans tended to run and hide whenever a '*gringo*' appeared, but he had rarely seen a place so deserted.

As ever, in situations like this, his senses were working overtime but in this instance they told him little. Brogan McNally, confessed saddletramp, was more at home out on the plains, the forest or the desert than in any town or village. Out there he could read the signs, hear the faintest of noises and know instantly what was happening; amongst houses those same sounds took on different meanings.

The only reason he was now riding along the rough, rutted street of this small Mexican town was that there had been little alternative, situated as it was at the end of a steep-sided pass. Another reason for not actually avoiding the town was that he was in need of a few supplies.

As was normal amongst the vast majority of Mexican settlements of anything more than half a dozen rough adobes, a gleaming, whitewashed church dominated, around which all main activity was centred, although in this case the wide square in front of the church was deserted. Even so, he could feel countless pairs of eyes staring at him from darkened windows.

Apart from the woman hurriedly rescuing her small child, there was one other sign that there were other human beings about, or rather six signs in the form of six horses, complete with saddles, tethered outside what appeared to be the sole building that was not a house or the church. Unconsciously

Brogan felt the handle of his Colt at his hip as he pulled up alongside the horses and glanced at a faded sign which proclaimed the building to be the cantina. It also appeared to be the general store and sole trading establishment.

Both he and horse seemed pleased to note that a trough of water occupied the length of the hitching rail and Brogan splashed himself, not because he felt dirty, just very hot. The horse looked disdainfully at its rider before lowering its muzzle and sampling the liquid as if uncertain that it was now in some way tainted.

The interior of the cantina was gratefully cool but dimly lit, although the six surly forms slouched across the solitary table in the centre of the room were quite unmistakably not the normal citizens of the town and it appeared to Brogan that he had stumbled across a meeting of the local *bandidos*. His first instinct was to turn and leave, but he knew from experience that such

3

an action would probably cause more trouble than if he stayed. The little man behind the bar, dressed more in keeping with a normal Mexican town dweller, looked nervously at the new arrival.

"*Señor*," the little man asked equally nervously, "What can I do for you?"

"A long, cool drink," replied Brogan turning his back on the six men at the table. "Don't suppose you have any beer."

"Beer? No, *señor*," apologized the man. "If it is a cool drink you are needing, then I have only lemonade. Very good lemonade," he hastened to add.

"Lemonade sounds just fine," nodded Brogan. The little man disappeared to return with an earthenware jug and a large, rather dirty looking glass which he looked at, smiled a little selfconsciously and proceeded to wipe on an even dirtier looking towel. Brogan did not complain, he had drunk out of dirtier things than that.

4

Glass in hand and taking a long pull on the liquid which, he was forced to admit, did indeed taste very good and very cold, Brogan casually looked about, his eyes now accustomed to the dim light and, without being too obvious, noted the exact position of every man around the table. From this one simple observation he was able to determine just which of the six was the leader. In this case it was quite obviously a seemingly tall — judging by the length of his outstretched leg — fairly slim, mustachioed and slightly more expensively dressed man, although, like his companions the expression on his face was surly to the point of being expressionless.

Beyond the men and the table Brogan could see what was plainly the general store part of the business. The six men continued to stare with seemingly lifeless eyes at the intruder and Brogan suddenly decided that he would like to take a look in the general store. Placing his glass down on the counter, he took the four steps which brought him almost face to face with the leader.

"Where you go, *gringo*?" came the harsh guttural tones of the leader although the only indication Brogan had that it had been he who spoke was that his up-to-now expressionless face now looked up at him.

"I need some supplies," said Brogan as he casually attempted to side-step the man's foot which had suddenly appeared in front of him. At the same time his hand dropped casually to his gun, unseen by the others.

The lips on the expressionless face moved. "Dead men do not need any supplies, *gringo*."

"I ain't dead yet," replied Brogan.

"One nod of my head and you are," rasped the Mexican. "I am the law in these parts, *gringo*. It is I who decides who lives and who dies."

Brogan gave a quick glance at the other five and his grip on the gun tightened. "Don't I have any say in the matter?" he asked with an apparent casualness that belied his readiness to act.

The Mexican laughed and changed his position slightly. "In this town Americanos are not welcome," he said. "Why do you come here?"

"Just passin' through," replied Brogan. "A man's got a right to pass through, ain't he?"

"You have no rights," came the guttural reply. "*Gringos* especially, they have no rights. You are in Mexico now and the only rights you have are what I choose to allow you."

"And just who the hell are you?" asked Brogan.

The Mexican seemed surprised at this question and again shifted his position. "You do not know, *gringo*?"

"Now that's a darned stupid question," sneered Brogan. "I wouldn't be askin' if I did, would I?"

For the first time the Mexican smiled thinly. "It is not good for you that you call me stupid. Nobody calls me, Pablo

Manuel Maria Hemenez, stupid."

"I didn't say you were stupid," Brogan pointed out. "All I said was it was a stupid question."

Pablo Manuel Maria Hemenez shrugged. "It is the same thing. I do not ask stupid questions. I ask you what you are doing here, I ask again."

"And I'll tell you again," replied Brogan, "I'm just passin' through."

"Why this town?" asked the Mexican. "Why you come this way? You are a long way from America. Why are you such a long way from America?"

"Why, is my business," said Brogan, "an' I didn't have much choice comin' through here. I had to; there was no way of avoidin' it bein' as it's at the end of the pass."

Pablo Manuel Maria Hemenez grinned and nodded. "*Si*, it is true, if you come through the pass you must go through the town." He suddenly sat up straight and stared at Brogan. "I tell you why you come here, *gringo*. You come here because you think that the army is here. You come here to give information to the army. I have heard that there are many Americanos who give information to the army of Mexico."

"Maybe so," agreed Brogan, "but this particular *gringo* ain't one of 'em. I guess I'm rather like you, I ain't too keen on meetin' the law either."

"Do not lie to me, *gringo*!" snarled the Mexican. "I know you come to give information to the army I think we should discover what that information is. What is it that you wish to tell the army? I advise you to answer. I can kill you just as easy as I can kill that cockroach on the floor." To accentuate his point his foot suddenly crashed down on a large cockroach which had unwittingly strayed across the floor. There was a crunch as the insect succumbed to the weight of the man's foot and to further accentuate his power, the Mexican slowly ground the remains into the dust and smiled threateningly.

"I ain't lyin'," replied Brogan.

Pablo Manuel Maria Hemenez sighed and shook his head. "It is unfortunate for you that nobody will miss you when you are dead, at least there is nobody to mourn your passing here in Mexico. If anyone should ask, the people of this town have not seen any *gringos* through here for many, many months."

The nod of his head was almost imperceptible in the dim light but it was enough for the other five *bandidos* to go for their guns.

Fortunately for Brogan and unfortunately for Pablo Manuel Maria Hemenez, they were all far too slow.

There was a mixture of gasps of disbelief and amazed grunts as the Mexican looked almost casually upwards at the barrel of Brogan's Colt now firmly pressing against his temple. Apart from the initial glance upwards, Pablo Manuel Maria Hemenez showed absolutely no emotion at all and even Brogan, who was rarely surprised by anything, was surprised at the man's apparent calmness.

"You are very quick with your gun, *gringo*," grinned the Mexican. "*Si*, I am very impressed. It looks to me like we now have what I understand you call in America as something of a Mexican standoff. *Si*, it is true that we are both in a position which is impossible for both of us, although I have never understood why such a situation should be given such a name. OK, *gringo*, so what do you do now? My men could kill you quite easily but would they be fast enough to stop you from killing me? It is an interesting question is it not?"

"Very interestin'," agreed Brogan. "The thing is there ain't no need for either or both of us to die, I'm sure neither of us wants that. Just tell your men to put their guns away an' I'll do the same. I don't know if they speak English or not, but I think they got the

11

message that I can handle both myself and this gun."

"They are ignorant pigs," grinned Hemenez. He spoke to his men in Spanish and they put away their guns, seeming almost relieved to do so.

"You chose your target very well, *gringo*," said Hemenez as Brogan too eased his Colt back into its holster. "Had you been foolish enough to choose any of my men, I would have had no hesitation in killing you even if it meant that you took the life of a useless pig." He laughed. "It is all right, *señor*, *si*, I feel you have earned the right for me to call you *señor*. They are all ignorant pigs and do not understand a word of English except the word 'dollar'. Most of them would sell their own mothers for just a few American dollars."

"And you?" asked Brogan.

Hemenez laughed. "Me! I have no mother alive to sell!" He laughed at what he thought was a joke.

"But you hate *gringos*," said Brogan.

"How do I know you won't try to kill me as soon as I turn my back?"

Hemenez laughed. "Then do not turn your back! I am naturally suspicious of all *gringos*, especially Americano *gringos*. The only reason they have come to this town before is to meet with the Mexican army. Sometimes they come to deliver messages and sometimes they come to deliver much needed gold . . . " Brogan looked surprised. "It is true. There are many people from Mexico and others in your country who make a great deal of money by keeping the army supplied and they do not wish to see an end to the troubles which ravage us at this moment."

"I guess that's what they call business," said Brogan.

Hemenez spat on to the floor and wiped his mouth. "It is their business to suppress the Mexican peon. In your country it is the black man, here it is the peon. The life of a peon is at the mercy of the landowners and the military. Their worth is less than that of the cockroach which I have just crushed under my foot. Do not speak to me about Americano businessmen."

It was plain that Pablo Manuel Maria Hemenez was a man with deep convictions and in a way Brogan admired him for those convictions, although he knew that there was absolutely nothing he could do about the situation and therefore did not want to become involved.

"Well you're quite wrong about this American *gringo*," he said. "All I was doin' was passin' through. I ain't got no interest or connection with the army or business."

"But why do you come to Mexico?" asked Hemenez.

"I like the place," said Brogan. "I like wide open spaces, the wind in my face and I even like the dry desert."

Hemenez smiled. "You are mad, just like all *gringos*. Very well, I believe what you say. You are free to go where you will."

By this time Brogan had lost interest in the general store, although he would buy some supplies later and he returned to his glass of lemonade, drank it and ordered a refill. The little cantina owner beamed happily As far as he was concerned all Americanos were very, very rich and this one would spend many dollars, although to him an American ten-dollar note was wealth indeed.

"Would you have had me killed?" Brogan asked as he picked up the second glass of lemonade and pushed a coin across the counter. The little man again beamed happily as he examined the coin. He did seem slightly disappointed that it proved to be a Mexican coin and not American, but he pocketed it and did not offer Brogan any change.

"Of course," came the casual reply "I do not make idle threats, it is a waste of breath to do so."

"Makes sense, I suppose," nodded Brogan. "Now, as I see it, you are in

15

control of this town right now, so what happened to the army?"

Hemenez laughed. "Yesterday the army was here, today we are here, tomorrow it may be the army again, the day after that . . . who knows? when the army come, unfortunately we must leave, that is the way things are; unfortunately we are not powerful enough to fight them or to prevent them coming."

"Don't the folk of this town have no say in the matter?"

"Not a lot," said Hemenez in a matter-of-fact way. "Did it not strike you that the town is very quiet?"

"I did notice," nodded Brogan, "but I thought that was just 'cos I rode in."

Hemenez smiled. "They have a natural suspicion of *gringos*," he agreed, "but that is not the main reason. Apart from our friend here . . . " He nodded at the cantina owner, "there are no more than ten men left in the town. That is because they have either been forced into service with the army, killed for refusing to do so or are now hiding out in the hills. Pedro here has only escaped because he has a badly injured leg and is not able to serve the soldiers. The other men are all too old."

As if in confirmation, Pedro rolled up the leg of his trousers to reveal a badly withered leg. He seemed almost proud of the fact.

"We do not like the soldiers," said Pedro. "They come into my cantina and drink everything but do not pay. Also they take any woman they choose and shoot anyone who tries to stop them."

"Looks like you've got problems," nodded Brogan. "I'm surprised the army don't take over the town permanently, it's in a good position."

Hemenez shrugged. "There was much talk about such a thing," he said, "but for some reason they chose not to do so. They seem quite happy to come when it pleases them."

"They come and you move out,"

said Brogan. "How many men are up in the hills?"

Hemenez thought for a moment. "Perhaps two hundred," he said. "I cannot be certain. I know what you are thinking, *gringo*. You are thinking why do they not fight the soldiers. You must remember that they are only peons, they are not trained to fight and they do not have the guns with which to fight. The people of your country are not interested in providing them with weapons since they cannot pay for them. They do the best they can. Sometimes they attack a small patrol and take their guns but each time they do this the soldiers take revenge on other peons."

"You look pretty well armed," observed Brogan.

Hemenez laughed. "We are different, *gringo*. In your country we would be called outlaws, here we are called *bandidos*."

"Outlaws steal from their own kind," said Brogan.

Hemenez shrugged. "We take what we need."

Brogan took another mouthful of lemonade, swilled it around his mouth for a moment and then swallowed it. "Seems to me that it's the peons who suffer either way," he said eventually "The soldiers come, take what they want and as many women as they want then you come in an' take what you want."

Hemenez laughed. "That is the way of things, *gringo*."

Brogan did not miss the very slight nod of the head as Hemenez spoke and a few seconds later two of his men left the cantina. He pretended not to notice. In some ways he quite liked Pablo Manuel Maria Hemenez, but then he also thought that a rattlesnake was a handsome animal, perfectly adapted for its lifestyle and safe enough if kept at a distance but deadly if you got too close.

Hemenez too seemed perfectly adapted to his environment. He was very calm, very self-assured and seemingly afraid of nothing. Brogan had to agree that there were a great many similarities between Hemenez and a rattlesnake.

"I'd say that the army would very much like to get their hands on you," said Brogan.

Hemenez smiled and pointed to a far wall where there were several notices. "A great many pesos," he said. "*Si*, perhaps like yourself I am worth a great deal more dead than alive."

Brogan smiled and shook his head. "That's where you an' me differ. I ain't worth nothin' to nobody, dead or alive."

Hemenez appeared slightly surprised. "A man who can use a gun like you do is usually wanted by someone somewhere."

"Not me," assured Brogan. "Believe this or not, as you choose, but this is one Americano hobo who ain't never stole nothin' off nobody in his life, ain't never raped a woman nor robbed a bank."

Hemenez studied Brogan for a moment. "But I see in your eyes that you have killed many men . . . yes, I think that you have killed many, many men."

"I done my share," admitted Brogan casually.

"Which makes you a very dangerous man, *gringo*," observed Hemenez. "Perhaps you are what you call a bounty hunter?"

"I've collected a few bounties from time to time," Brogan agreed, "but I don't make a habit of it, only when it suits."

"Perhaps you are even now thinking of the reward there is on me and my men?"

"Didn't know there was until you mentioned it."

Hemenez smiled. "But I did mention it so now you are thinking about it."

"Could be that I am," goaded Brogan. "Only trouble is I wouldn't know how to go about collectin' it in Mexico."

Hemenez suddenly laughed. "At least

you are honest, *gringo*. Every other *gringo* I have met has never been honest with me. I can trust a man who is honest with me."

"Even if I want to turn you in?"

"Even that," laughed Hemenez. "Just as I would not hesitate to kill you if it suited me. It is good that we both know this, it means there is a certain respect between us."

"Respect is one thing," said Brogan, "trust is another. I hope you don't mind if I don't share your trust."

"Is it for me to mind? What you think is your business, *gringo*, just as my mind is for me to think what I want."

Brogan smiled. "Just puttin' things straight. Anyhow, it don't really matter that much, I don't intend hangin' about. I'll just pick up a few things an' be on my way."

Hemenez smiled and nodded as Brogan made his way to the door where he paused briefly on the pretext of feeling in his shirt pocket but in reality his eagle eyes were weighing up the situation outside.

Through a crack in the rickety wooden door, Brogan could see the two men apparently lounging against the wall, facing his way and, although he could not see their hands, he was able to see that their guns were missing from their holsters. He casually opened the door . . .

* * *

His reaction was experienced and honed on practice: before the two men realized exactly what was happening, Brogan rolled out of the door and bounced to his feet, gun drawn and already firing, two yards away. Both men howled in pain and their guns fell harmlessly into the dust. They each stared in pure disbelief as Brogan moved swiftly to one side to put one of their horses between him and the door. As expected, the other three men came running out, guns drawn but unable to shoot. Hemenez himself ambled out a few seconds later and looked with disgust at the two injured men. He motioned the others to put their guns away.

"I should have expected nothing less, *gringo*," he laughed. "I was right, you have killed many men and are very dangerous. Tell me, why did you not kill these two useless pigs?"

"Maybe it was just bad shootin'," replied Brogan.

"No, *señor*, I think not," said Hemenez.

2

IN most other circumstances the sound of gunfire would have brought inquisitive onlookers, all at safe distance of course, but on this occasion there was almost total silence. Almost but not quite. A small, brown-robed figure appeared briefly at the door of the church but the appearance was very brief although not unnoticed by Brogan.

The two injured *bandidos* were examining their seemingly shattered hands which, on closer examination were not as badly injured as the amount of blood made it appear. If anything was really injured it was their pride.

Hemenez spoke to his men in Spanish and although they all grumbled, they trooped back into the cantina leaving the Americano to tend to his horse.

Brogan found what he thought was a bag of horsefeed against the cantina wall — which turned out to be corn seed — opened it and laid it in front of the animal. Whilst he was doing this he glanced towards the church where once again he caught a glimpse of a shadowy figure.

Checking briefly that Hemenez and his *bandidos* were still inside the cantina, Brogan casually wandered across the square to the church where, in the very cool interior, there was no sign of the brown robed figure.

However, Brogan knew that it had not been his imagination and a glance around the church told him that whoever it was must still be inside since there were no other exits, or so it seemed. He moved slowly forward between the rows of rough wooden benches which served as pews towards the ornate altar.

As ever, it appeared to Brogan that no matter how poor the Mexican people appeared to be, they spared no expense when it came to decorating their churches. Not being a religious man himself — in fact he was not too sure what he believed — he had always considered the expense lavished on such churches would be far better spent on the poor but, such was their choice and he had to concede their right to do as they wanted.

He went around the back of the altar, gun at the ready just in case since he had known devoutly religious men shoot first and think later, and suddenly threw back a cloth which hung down the back to reveal the cowering, brown-robed figure he had seen at the door.

"Afternoon, Padre," he smiled. "I don't speak no Spanish, I hope you speak English." The terrified figure nodded briefly but stayed where he was. Brogan glanced at his gun, smiled and put it away. "You can come out, Padre, I don't mean you no harm."

The figure seemed a little better assured now that this tall, dirty, *gringo* had put his gun away and slowly uncoiled himself, eventually to stand alongside Brogan and stare up at him with a certain amount of awe.

"Welcome to Santa Cruz," croaked the padre. "I am, Padre Miguel."

"Santa Cruz!" mused Brogan. "Fancy name for a two-bit town."

The padre smiled weakly. "It is not a name chosen by me," he said. "There is a much larger Santa Cruz in another part of Mexico. I cannot help thinking that you are either very lucky or a man with much influence since you are still alive after meeting Señor Hemenez. It is well known that he hates all *gringos*, especially Americano *gringos*."

"Is it that obvious I'm American?" grinned Brogan.

"In this part of Mexico we hardly ever see any others," nodded Padre Miguel. "You are very fast with your gun, *señor*, but I am still surprised that Señor Hemenez allowed you to live."

"It could be that he's in the cantina plannin' my death right now," grinned

Brogan. "Why did you hide from me?"

"I . . . I . . . although I am a priest, *señor*, I have little faith in my fellow men these days. I have long since learned that few can be trusted, be they Americans or Mexicans."

"Not even Hemenez or the soldiers?"

Padre Miguel laughed weakly. "The soldiers, they apologize for raping the women and stealing the food but they come back a few days later and apologize once again. They also apologize when they kill someone but say it was necessary. Señor Hemenez at least is more honest, he does not apologize for anything. Even so the women and the children must suffer."

By this time the pair were walking towards the entrance to the church where they were suddenly faced by two women who almost screamed when they saw Brogan, but Padre Miguel managed to quieten them down.

"It is all right," he assured, "I have come to no harm."

The older of the two women stared

29

at Brogan for a while. "The shooting, Padre, we heard the shooting and we thought . . . !"

Padre Miguel smiled and laid his arm gently on the woman's shoulder. "I am pleased that you talk in English so that our guest can understand. It is all right, he means no harm." He turned to Brogan. "Allow me to introduce Maria Gonzales, her husband is the head man in the town."

"Is?" queried Brogan. "I thought most of the men had taken to the hills."

"*Si*, that is so," agreed the padre, "but her husband is too old to interest the soldiers." He ushered the two women towards the door where the younger woman suddenly spoke.

"You must be a very brave man to face Señor Hemenez," she said. "There are few who would stand against him."

"Maybe it ain't so much bein' brave as bein' plain foolish," grinned Brogan.

She looked at him smilingly. "No, I think not foolish. My brother Manuel, he was foolish when he stood against Señor Hemenez and his men. He is now dead, killed by the big one they call El Torro, the bull, killed with his bare hands. It is a pity you did not kill El Torro."

Brogan had noted that one of the men he had injured was indeed a huge, hairy monster of a man and he could well imagine him killing people with his bare hands just for pleasure.

"You saw what happened just now?"

"*Si*, I saw," she smiled. "That is why I do not think you are foolish. I only wish I could be so brave, I would kill El Torro to avenge my brother."

"My child," soothed Padre Miguel, "it is sinful to even think of revenge. Be assured that the Good Lord will exact justice when the time comes for El Torro to meet Him."

"*Si*, I understand that, Padre," she whispered. "It is just that I would like to give him the pleasure of begging the Good Lord for forgiveness before he is much older."

Padre Miguel hid a smile from her as he ushered them through the door and when he turned he was having to choke back a laugh. "I forgive her, her brother was only six years old." He became more serious. "The boy managed to get hold of a gun which he pointed at El Torro. You must remember that he was only a little boy and that the gun was very ancient and not loaded. El Torro however, became much enraged, grabbed the boy by the neck and swung him round, much as a dog will do with a cat or rabbit. I do not think the boy suffered much, his neck was broken."

"He sounds a nice character," nodded Brogan.

Padre Miguel looked a little oddly at Brogan and then smiled thinly. "*Si*, I see that you jest, *señor*, but it is not really a matter for laughter."

"Sorry," apologized Brogan, "I didn't mean it to sound like that."

"I realize that," smiled the padre. "However, I now fear for your life. Señor Hemenez is not known for his kindness and he does not like to think that anyone could get the better of him."

Brogan smiled. "I shouldn't worry 'bout what happens to me, Padre. It seems you've got enough problems. I've heard stories about how the soldiers treat the people but I wasn't sure if that's all they were, stories."

Padre Miguel nodded his head sagely. "Stories? *Si*, there are many stories but unfortunately they are all true. Many months ago I was visiting Mexico City and even there they believe such things to be no more than stories. In Mexico City the people have great contempt for the peons of the countryside; they do not understand."

Brogan sighed and shook his head. He knew that he was always a sucker for the hard-luck tale and often ended up fighting for whomsoever he considered the underdog, but even he knew that he could not take on the whole military might of a nation.

"I wish there was somethin' I could

do," he said, "but there ain't, you must know that."

The padre smiled sympathetically. "Such is the lot of the peon," he said. "There is nothing anyone can do; even the Church is powerless and I sometimes think that the bishops too do not care about the plight of the people."

The daylight at the church door was suddenly broken as a tall figure stood there, silhouetted against the brightness. Brogan's hand automatically rested on the handle of his gun but he did not draw.

"You pray for forgiveness, *gringo*?" laughed the silhouette. "Perhaps you should also pray for your soul."

"The only prayin' I've ever done is crouchin' on one knee behind a gun," retorted Brogan.

"And I see that your prayers have always been answered," laughed Hemenez moving into the coolness of the church. "One day, *gringo*, your prayers will not be answered. I come to tell you that the soldiers they are coming and that it is time for us to leave. I suggest that you too leave while you can, the soldiers too are not bothered if they kill Americanos. Even if they do not, it would be safer for you if you are not here when me and my men return. The two men you shot are very angry, they do not like it when someone shows them for what they are, lumbering pigs. They have both vowed to kill you."

"Thanks for the warning," said Brogan. "So the soldiers are coming back; how do you know?"

Hemenez laughed. "The men you see with me are not the only ones. I always send at least two men to keep a look-out for the return of the soldiers. Did you not hear one ride into town just now?"

Brogan shook his head and had to admit that he had not, which annoyed him slightly since he prided himself in being able to hear things that other people could not; but this time his ability seemed to have deserted him.

"You too must leave, *señor*," urged the priest. "Señor Hemenez is quite right; they are as likely to kill you on sight as they would anyone."

"Suddenly everyone's concerned about me," mused Brogan. "It sure makes a nice change; normally nobody could give a damn about me or what happens to me."

"It is for your own safety, *señor*," the priest urged again.

"Listen to the priest," laughed Hemenez. "I can assure you that I too do not give a damn what happens to you, but it would seem to be a waste of time since I could so easily have killed you myself and gained some pleasure from doing so. You are a man after my own heart, *gringo*, that is the only reason you are alive, but do not expect me to control my men."

"I hear what you say," said Brogan. "How soon will they be here?"

"No more than one hour," grinned Hemenez. "Now I must go; there is nothing they would like better than to get their hands on me."

Brogan was tempted to wish the *bandido* the best of luck but said nothing as Hemenez ran from the church towards his horse.

"I too must go and warn everyone that they come," said the padre. "If nothing else they will be prepared and the little ones can be hidden away."

"The little ones?" queried Brogan.

"*Si*," nodded Padre Miguel sadly. "Even the smallest child is not beyond being molested by the soldiers. At least Hemenez and his men do not treat the children in this way."

"No," said Brogan, "they just kill 'em."

Padre Miguel smiled weakly and hurried from the church, almost breaking into a run but not quite, as if such a thing would be a little too undignified for a man of the cloth.

Brogan ambled from the church across the dusty square to the cantina where he discovered the owner hurriedly transferring his more valuable stock into a hidden cellar. He saw Brogan and smiled.

"I have not the time to sell you anything, *señor*, I must hide what I can and only leave the cheapest drink and food. Perhaps if you are still alive when they leave . . . "

"I'll do my best to see that I am," grinned Brogan. "Seems to me that it's hardly worth your while takin' that stuff out of there when they've gone."

Pedro grinned. "Sometimes that is the way of things, *señor*. This time they return quickly, it was only four days ago that they were here. It is usually at least two weeks. Something must have happened to make them return so soon."

Brogan helped himself to a large peach from a bowl at the back of the counter and wandered back on to the square to consider his next move. He bit into the fruit and wiped the juice from around his mouth before speaking to his horse.

"Can't see why the soldiers should bother about us, old girl," he said to her. "What you wanna do, stay here for a while?" The horse shook her head and Brogan smiled. "One of these days you an' me is goin' to agree on somethin'. OK, we go, there ain't much sense in invitin' trouble." His horse nodded her head this time. Again Brogan smiled. "If I didn't know better, I'd say you understood every darned word I say." He mounted up and swung her round. "OK, let's go. Hemenez and his men went that way I guess that's the opposite way from the soldiers so that's the way we go."

* * *

Brogan had ridden about four miles from the town when he heard them, the unmistakable sound of hooves, quite a lot of them. Normally he would have pulled off the trail and hidden to allow whoever it was to pass by. This time however, there was absolutely nowhere

39

that a man could hide, let alone a man and his horse.

The shallow valley was about two miles wide and completely barren, there was not even any cactus and what few large rocks there were were too far away. Whoever was approaching was hidden from view by quite a steep rise across the valley floor but even that was too far away for Brogan to make use of. He sighed, patted the neck of his horse and resigned himself to meeting what sounded increasingly like possible trouble.

He was not at all surprised when a body of Mexican soldiers appeared over the rise, but they seemed very surprised to see him and the officer in command raised his hand to call his men to a halt.

It was not the officer who approached Brogan, but a man of lesser rank, apparently a sergeant. The sergeant took his time in coming towards this unexpected stranger and he looked harshly as if uncertain whether this disreputable stranger was human.

He spoke to Brogan in Spanish and although the question was quite plain in any language, Brogan shrugged his shoulders. The sergeant slowly circled Brogan as if checking every unbelievable detail before speaking again. "Americano?" he rasped harshly Brogan nodded. The sergeant made another circle. "Why you come here, Americano, where you go, where you come from?"

"I'm headin' back to America," said Brogan.

"America?" laughed the sergeant. He called to his officer in Spanish who then rode forward and addressed Brogan in perfect English.

"You claim to be heading to America," said the officer. "Then why are you on this road?"

Brogan shrugged. "This ain't the way?" he said.

The officer smiled indulgently. "No, *señor*, this is not the way to America."

"Then I'm lost," said Brogan.

41

The officer smiled and nodded. "Indeed you are lost, *señor*, or are you? You have the look of a man who is well used to finding his way around the countryside. No, *señor*, I do not think you are lost. Why do you come this way?"

Brogan smiled and decided that he was not going to fool this young officer very easily. "I was tryin' to avoid you," he finally admitted.

If the officer was surprised he did not show it. "You were attempting to avoid the army? At least that sounds an honest answer but it is nevertheless a puzzling one and raises many questions." Brogan had realized it had not been the wisest thing to say almost as soon as he said it. "The obvious question it raises in my mind," continued the officer, "is why you should be so anxious to avoid us. If you have nothing to hide then you have nothing to fear and no reason to wish to avoid us. However, the next question it raises is how did you know that the military were in the area?"

"I was warned," admitted Brogan.

"You were warned!" mused the officer. "That is most interesting. By whom were you warned and why?"

"Some *bandido* called Hemenez," Brogan admitted deciding that honesty was probably the best way to extract himself from a tricky situation. Again, if the officer was surprised he did not show it.

"Hemenez!" said the officer. "You are a friend of Señor Hemenez perhaps?"

"Never met him before today," said Brogan. "I'd never heard of him before."

"You have never met Pablo Manuel Maria Hemenez before in your life but suddenly he tells you there are soldiers coming and advises you to come this way? I find that very strange, *señor*. Your name, *señor*?" The officer became quite serious.

"McNally," said Brogan. "Brogan McNally."

"McNally," said the officer. "Your

occupation Mr McNally?"

"Occupation?" grinned Brogan trying to sound casual. "I ain't got no occupation. I'm what we call a saddletramp, what you would call . . . "

"I am well aware what a saddletramp is, Mr McNally," interrupted the officer. "As you no doubt can tell, I speak perfect English and even American. I was born in England and attended an English university although both my parents were Mexican. I have also studied in New York and have travelled much of America."

"I'd never've guessed it," mumbled Brogan.

"Sarcasm does not become you," smiled the officer. "Now, Mr McNally, I repeat my question: Why do you come this way?"

"I've already told you," replied Brogan. "I was trying to avoid you."

"A most unsatisfactory answer, Mr McNally," smiled the officer. "I would strongly advise you to be more co-operative — I can assure you that all

44

I have to do is nod to any of my men and you will be shot and I can also assure you that nobody will bother to investigate your death."

Brogan knew that the officer spoke the truth. He could be killed as easily as Hemenez had crushed the cockroach and nobody would bother. He had been in tight spots before but this particular situation had the makings of becoming impossible to get out of. By telling the truth he raised other, quite legitimate, questions and by telling lies he was likely to be found out and punished for it. Had these men been *bandidos* or outlaws he would have no hesitation in attempting to shoot his way out of trouble, but these were not a disorganized rabble, they were highly trained and disciplined men, looking even more disciplined than most Mexican soldiers he had encountered. He knew these were some elite troop.

Brogan shrugged. "Either way I can't win. I tell the truth an' I'm not believed an' if I tell you some story I wouldn't be believed."

The officer laughed. "I can appreciate your problem, Mr McNally. Under the circumstances I think the matter can only be resolved by someone with greater authority than I have. Hand your guns and any knife you may have over to the sergeant and we shall carry on to Santa Cruz where, by now, Colonel Sanchez should have arrived. Colonel Sanchez is the local military governor."

"I've got a better idea," said Brogan, more in hope than serious suggestion, "why don't you just forget all about me, pretend you haven't seen me? I won't say nothin'. All I want is to get back to America. After all, I'm nobody, I'm just a no-good saddletramp."

"I tend to agree that you are a nobody, Mr McNally," smiled the officer, "I believe you are what you claim to be, nothing more than a saddletramp. However, I cannot be certain. I cannot be certain that you are not a spy or that you have been sent to assassinate someone. Such things have happened before."

"Assassinate!" exclaimed Brogan. "Does that mean kill someone?" The officer nodded. "Kill who?" continued Brogan. "I don't know anyone an' don't have no grudge against nobody in Mexico."

The officer laughed. "Again, I believe you, but I dare not take the chance. There is a very important dignitary due here soon, someone many of my countrymen and quite a lot of yours would like to have killed. I am sorry, Mr McNally but you must come with us. Please hand over your weapons at once and without further argument. You have less than one minute, Mr McNally after that you will be shot."

A quick look into the cold, calculating eyes of the young officer was enough. Brogan handed over his guns and his knife.

3

LIEUTENANT Luis Del Marco Granta, as Brogan soon discovered the young officer was named, seemed almost relieved when Brogan handed over his weapons and he nodded approvingly.

"Very wise, *señor*," he said slipping back into the Mexican way of speaking. "I am quite sure that before long you will be on your way back to America. Colonel Sanchez is a fair man, not at all the monster many would have you believe."

"I ain't never heard of him," said Brogan.

The lieutenant laughed. "I would not tell him so," he advised. "He may be a fair man but he also very vain. It will not please him to think that someone has never heard of him."

"Thanks for the information," said

Brogan. "Anythin' else I ought to know?"

"Just tell the truth," smiled the lieutenant. "It is always the wisest thing to do when talking to the colonel, he can somehow sense when someone is lying to him. It would also be very wise from your own point of view. Colonel Sanchez takes great delight in having the truth extracted from a liar. I can assure you they always end up telling the truth."

Brogan had met Colonel Sanchez before, under different names and guises and often persuading people to tell the truth when they knew the truth had already been told.

"Does he have a grudge against *gringos*?" asked Brogan.

"*Gringos* . . . no," the lieutenant grinned sardonically "Americanos . . . *si*!"

Brogan shook his head and gave a derisory laugh. "That makes me feel a whole lot better!"

★ ★ ★

Lieutenant Granta's troop arrived in Santa Cruz at exactly the same time as another, much larger body of soldiers. The lieutenant and his men arrived from the south and the others from the north, having come through the pass. Lieutenant Granta gave instructions to his sergeant who in turn barked an order at two soldiers who strode over to Brogan, guns at the ready and looking almost eager to use them. They spoke to Brogan in Spanish, of which he could not understand a word but knew very well what was said. He obeyed what he thought were the instructions and dismounted. Immediately both soldiers closed in behind him and prodded him in the back, which Brogan interpreted as a painful instruction to walk.

He walked and was guided into the cantina where the owner looked sympathetically at him but did not speak. It was obvious that the little room at the back of the store into which he was pushed, was one frequently used by the soldiers to detain prisoners.

The room was small, no more than five feet square, completely bare and, when the door was slammed shut and bolted, totally dark. In fact it had been a very long time since Brogan had experienced such complete blackness, not even the faintest hint of light showed through either the door or the doorway.

Brogan was no stranger to unsavoury smells, but he soon became very aware that should the call of nature come, there was only one place to relieve oneself as others had plainly done so many times before his confinement.

If he was unable to see anything, he was certainly able to hear many things, chief of which was the sound of soldiers entering the cantina and demanding food and drink. Such words seem to translate readily in any language. He heard the word *gringo* many times and it was obvious that he was the topic of discussion and more than once one of them banged heavily on the stout door and called out to him. He chose to ignore them which seemed to annoy them and he half hoped that they would become so annoyed that they would break down the door, but that was not to be.

★ ★ ★

Brogan was well used to assessing how much time had passed under normal conditions, but the total darkness had the effect of making time meaningless. He knew that he had slept, curled up in a corner, but for how long he had no idea and it almost appeared that they had forgotten all about him. But he was quite sure that they had not and that he would be dragged back into daylight very soon.

However, he had almost reached the point of calling out and demanding that he be released when the bolts were drawn back noisily and the door flung open and even the dim light of the interior of the cantina was unbearable.

He was dragged roughly from the room and pushed out into the square, but by that time his eyes had become accustomed to the daylight.

"Good morning, Mr McNally," smiled the familiar face of Lieutenant Granta. "I trust you slept well."

"Slept well!" exclaimed Brogan glancing up at the clear sky. One glance was enough to tell him that almost a whole day had passed since he had been locked up. However, he was not going to admit to anyone that he had lost track of time. "Yes, thanks," he continued.

"The accommodation was a bit sparse and the room service was non-existent, but I slept pretty good. What took you a whole darned day?"

The lieutenant smiled. "You obviously know how long you have been locked up. I must admit that you are the first man I have come across who seemed to know. Yes, Mr McNally, you have been confined for a little under twenty-four hours. It is normal procedure, it usually makes prisoners rather more talkative. Has it made you more talkative, Mr McNally?" He answered his own question. "No, somehow I do not think that it has. You struck me as a man who, while outwardly being nothing more than a saddletramp, is a man well used to privations and more than capable of looking after himself. In fact I would go so far as to say that you are not afraid of dying."

"It don't bother me," admitted Brogan. "That don't mean I'm over-anxious to try it out though. I'm quite happy with this life."

"Perhaps it is not the dying but the method of dying?"

"Dead is dead," smiled Brogan.

"How very true," said the lieutenant. "Come, Mr McNally, Colonel Sanchez wishes to talk to you."

Two soldiers closed behind Brogan as he followed Lieutenant Granta across the dusty square towards an adobe which was slightly larger than the others and proved to be the priest's house. On the way across the square the priest, standing in the doorway of his church, nodded briefly but otherwise ignored him, as did the older woman he had met in the church the previous day Colonel Sanchez was a rather overweight man, sloppily dressed which was in complete contrast to Lieutenant Granta and even the men under his command. That was another thing Brogan had noticed as they had crossed the square. The men under the command of the lieutenant quite plainly kept themselves apart from the other soldiers and certainly seemed to take more pride in their appearance.

The lieutenant snapped smartly to attention and saluted his superior who almost grudgingly managed to raise a finger as salute in return and studiously busied himself with some papers as if deliberately keeping both the lieutenant and the prisoner waiting. Lieutenant Granta was plainly used to such treatment and stayed rigidly at attention. Eventually Colonel Sanchez lowered a paper he had been studying and spoke.

"This is the prisoner?" he asked in English, which rather surprised Brogan.

"Yes, sir," replied Lieutenant Granta. "He claims his name is Brogan McNally."

The colonel stared at Brogan for a while, looking him up and down. "Is that your name?" he demanded.

"Only one I ever had," replied Brogan. "It ain't much but it's all mine."

"You would be well advised to be a little less flippant in your reply," advised the colonel. He picked up another piece of paper and studied it for a moment. "I have here the report from Lieutenant Granta and as usual it is a very precise report . . ." He said that with obvious sarcasm. "You claim you were deliberately trying to avoid the military. Tell me, Mr McNally, why should you wish to do this? It must be that you have something to hide or in some way fear the military."

"Let's just say I like to keep away from authority." said Brogan. "We never seem to see eye to eye."

"But surely if you have done nothing wrong there is no need to fear any authority."

"Experience tells me that isn't always the case," said Brogan. "Not just here in Mexico but in America as well."

The colonel looked him up and down again and grunted. "You have the appearance of what you claim to be, a hobo, and you certainly have the smell but there is just one small thing which puzzles me and it also appears to puzzle the lieutenant as well. Why did the *bandido*, Hemenez, not have you killed? I find that most puzzling, yes indeed." He sighed with obvious disbelief. "The only thing Hemenez and I have in common is a mutual dislike of Americano *gringos*. I will not bore you with the reason but I do not deny my dislike and I know that Hemenez has an even greater hatred.

That is what I find so puzzling. I have never known Hemenez allow any *gringo* to live, but suddenly . . . " He spread his arms and shrugged, "he has plainly allowed you your life." Again he shrugged. "I am bound to say that I actually believe your story, that you have met him. Please explain to my simple mind why he should do this?"

"Mainly 'cos I'm faster with a gun than any of his men," smiled Brogan.

The colonel gazed at the disreputable figure before him and nodded. "*Si*, you have the look of a gunfighter. I think that at least Hemenez would respect you for that."

"He did try to kill me, or have me killed, twice," said Brogan. "The first time was in the cantina and the second outside. I reckon the cantina owner could confirm it, he must have seen what happened."

"It is true, Colonel," said the lieutenant. "I have already questioned the owner of the cantina. He confirms McNally's story and says he has never seen a man act so swiftly."

The colonel grunted. "Hemenez is supposed to be very fast with a pistol," he said. "Are you even faster than he is?"

"Wouldn't know," said Brogan. "It was his men who tried to kill me, not him."

"Do you not think it would be interesting to find out?" asked the colonel, smiling for the first time.

"Can't say as I'm that keen to find out," said Brogan. "So far I've managed pretty well, but one of these days I'm sure to come against someone who is better'n me. I ain't in no hurry to meet that feller yet though."

The colonel almost laughed. "Very wise. It is indeed a wise man who knows what his limits are." He glared harshly at Brogan. "You are a wise man are you not?"

"Most folk'd say I was plain stupid sometimes," smiled Brogan.

The smile seemed to annoy the colonel who slammed his fist on to the table. "I did not ask what others think of you!" he roared. "I asked you if you think you are a wise man."

"I try to be," replied Brogan.

"You try to be!" grated the colonel. "Then try to be a wise man now, *gringo*. Why should Hemenez allow you to live? What are you doing here? Who sent you? Answer truthfully, I will know if you are lying to me."

Brogan gave a quick glance at Lieutenant Granta but he was showing no emotion at all. "I can only repeat that it was because I was faster than his men with a gun," he said. "There's no other reason I can think of. What am I doing here? Just like I told the lieutenant, I just happened to be passin' through. I came through the pass and couldn't avoid the town. Who sent me? Nobody sent me, why should they? I'm a saddletramp and I go wherever the fancy takes me, includin' Mexico sometimes."

The colonel smiled and picked on one point. "Why should anyone send you? Yes indeed why should anyone send you?" He leaned forward and glared up at Brogan. "I will tell you why someone should send you here. This afternoon we have a very important official visiting the area and it is well known that the *bandidos* and certain members of your government would like to see this particular official assassinated." He sat back and smiled with smug satisfaction. "I think, Mr McNally, that we have the answer as to why Hemenez did not kill you. You were sent here to assassinate this official and that it plainly suited the purpose of Hemenez to allow you to do so. His hands would be clean, he could quite properly claim that it was an Americano who carried out the assassination, always assuming you would have succeeded."

"I've gotta admit you make it sound quite logical," said Brogan. "Only trouble is it just ain't so. I don't know nothin' 'bout no official comm' here an' I doubt very much if the name would mean anythin' to me if I heard it."

"Have you ever heard my name?" asked the colonel puffing his chest out slightly.

Brogan remembered Lieutenant Granta's warning that the colonel was a vain man.

"Nope!" he replied, completely ignoring the advice. "First time I've ever been in these parts."

Colonel Sanchez was obviously shocked but he suddenly relaxed and sat back. "At least you appear to be honest, Mr McNally. It takes either a very honest man or a very foolish one to say that he has never heard of me, Colonel Enrico Sanchez, Military Governor of this province and I do not think you are a foolish man, unwise perhaps, but foolish . . . no." He looked at the lieutenant and smiled. "I think that perhaps the lieutenant advised you to admit to knowing who I was. Lieutenant Granta is a very fine officer and in command of one of our finest units and it is said that his loyalty is beyond question. All I know is that he is indeed a fine officer but I also know that he is probably more English than Mexican, having spent his youth in England."

"Nobody's perfect," smiled Brogan.

"Indeed not," agreed the colonel. "Unfortunately I do not have the time to question you further. Our visitor will be here very soon and we must be ready for him. I do not wish for him to see that we have an American prisoner, you will be kept locked up until he has departed."

"I've got a better idea," grinned Brogan, "you just point me in any direction you like an' I'll just keep on ridin'. That way we'll save us both a whole lot of trouble."

"Trouble, Mr McNally?" responded the colonel sharply. "Are you expecting trouble? Could it be that you do indeed know far more than you are admitting? I think perhaps so. I was going to order that you be kept in the room

63

at the cantina but now I think that your tongue needs to be loosened." He glared at Lieutenant Granta and spoke to him in Spanish. Although Brogan could not speak or understand the language, the tone of what the colonel said filled him with a lot of foreboding.

Lieutenant Granta's face remained expressionless as he acknowledged what was plainly an order, saluted and turned. The two soldiers behind Brogan prodded him in the back which he took to mean that he was to follow the lieutenant.

Outside, Lieutenant Granta spoke to Brogan with a tinge of sadness. "I had thought that you were a wise man," he said, "but it was very foolish of you to suggest to the colonel that trouble could be avoided if he released you. I am sorry, Mr McNally, I truly am, but unfortunately for you your next few hours are not going to be very pleasant."

"Worse than that room at the

cantina?" asked Brogan.

"*Si, señor*," replied the lieutenant gravely "Much worse!"

★ ★ ★

The meaning behind Lieutenant Granta's words became crystal clear a few minutes later when Brogan was led about a hundred yards away from the town towards a low, dust-covered tin shed standing alone. Brogan had heard of such things before and heard of their use in America and some American prisons. There they were commonly known as 'sweat boxes'.

His hands were bound, although he knew that he would have little difficulty in freeing himself and then he was pushed inside the tin shed where, to his dismay, he was lashed firmly to a short post and his ankles tied. The bonds around his wrists were reinforced by other lashings and eventually the tin door was slammed shut. Activity outside and noises on the tin roof indicated that all the dust was being swept off the roof to allow the hot sun to have a better effect on the metal. There were shouts from the two soldiers followed by laughter and, through the crack in the door, he could see the soldiers sauntering back to the town.

The action of the sun on the metal was very swift and within a very short period of time Brogan discovered that to struggle against his bonds simply made matters worse. Minutes turned agonizingly slowly into an hour and the heat of the day intensified as noon approached. Brogan struggled, not against his bonds but against the feeling that he was dying . . .

★ ★ ★

Voices! Somewhere over his head Brogan could hear voices but try as he might he could not locate the precise source. His arms moved and a searing pain racked his body and he stopped moving. Suddenly something very cold slithered down his throat, a throat parched and swollen to an extent which made it almost impossible to swallow. The effect of the cold liquid was to make his body lurch in agony as it rebelled. He turned, despite the agony it caused and wretched into the dust.

He was vaguely conscious of being turned on to his back and having his head raised again but this time the intense heat and light from above seemed less severe. Once again something was placed to his lips and there was the sensation of coldness in his mouth and throat. This time however, although his body rebelled, he did manage to keep the liquid in his mouth and after a time he felt better for it.

The voices were there again only this time one of them sounded different, softer, gentle and soothing. His eyes hurt but he did manage to open them and focus very briefly upon the young woman he had met inside the church.

She smiled briefly and wiped a cool cloth across his forehead.

She spoke to someone nearby in Spanish and then to Brogan who had been forced to close his eyes again. "All will be well, *señor*," she whispered. "You are safe now."

Brogan wanted to ask where he was and what had happened but he never discovered if he actually said anything or not. His eyes opened briefly again and this time he saw another figure alongside the woman, a figure dressed in the brown robes of a priest. He relaxed, sensing that all would be well, as the woman had said.

★ ★ ★

"Breakfast, *señor*!" announced the priest bearing down on Brogan with a bowl in one hand and a mug in the other. "It is not much, a little soup and bread and some coffee."

"Coffee sounds fine," croaked Brogan, his throat sore and seemingly swollen.

"Don't know about soup though."

"You must eat," insisted the priest, "your body needs food."

Brogan had been awake only a few minutes before Padre Miguel came in and he had not had time to assess his surroundings properly but with the padre came a shaft of daylight which confirmed that he was actually in the church and at the rear of the altar.

"How did I get out?" Brogan asked. "Out of that tin hell-hole?"

Padre Miguel smiled and helped Brogan to sit up. "For that you must give thanks to Lieutenant Granta."

"Granta?" queried Brogan, taking the mug of coffee in his trembling hands.

"*Si*," the padre nodded. "He is a good man; not all soldiers are bad, but they must obey orders, we all understand this. Colonel Sanchez and the minister have departed for another town and the lieutenant has been left in command at Santa Cruz. It is only temporary, the colonel and the minister are due back here tomorrow. Lieutenant Granta ordered your release almost as soon as the colonel had departed."

Brogan's mind was still in something of a turmoil but things were rapidly falling into place. "My grateful thanks to the lieutenant." He tried to smile but realized that it must have had more the appearance of a painful grimace, which it was. "Minister! What minister?"

The padre smiled. "He is the important official who was expected, the minister responsible for the army and law and order."

This time Brogan did manage a wry smile. "What law and order?"

Padre Miguel also smiled. "I understand what you mean, *señor*. *Si*, there are many times when even I despair about such things. Hemenez comes and goes as he pleases, although it must be said that he is popular among the peons. The army too come and go as they please, raping and looting as they see fit. Although they are officially the instrument of the law, they are not popular."

"Well at least Lieutenant Granta seems more human than most."

"This is true," agreed the priest, "but he is still a soldier and there is not one man or woman I know of who would not kill him for that fact alone but, as you say, he does have a little more respect and humanity. In fairness to him he will not allow his soldiers to do many of the things other soldiers do. His is a special unit, only the very best soldiers are selected and the discipline is very strict, but they are still soldiers."

Brogan changed the subject after drinking the coffee. "How long was I in that hut?"

"Only a few hours," grinned the priest. "It was about ten in the morning when you were locked up and you were taken out at four in the evening." He laughed. "Just long enough for your flesh to start cooking but not long enough for you to be served up on the plate. I have seen the hut used many times before and almost always the victim dies. Usually he is brought out dead and, as horrible as it may seem, well cooked. Others are brought out alive and die soon afterwards and a few, such as you, manage to survive. The longest I have known a man be in there and live is ten hours. You managed six hours, I do not think you could have survived even another hour."

"I must have passed out early on," said Brogan. "How long have I been here?"

"Since you were removed from the hut, all day yesterday and until now. It is now about ten in the morning."

Brogan shook his head. "That means I've been out for two days! It don't seem like two hours."

"*Si*, two days," agreed the priest. "In that time the whole town has been praying for you and their prayers have been answered."

"Prayin' for me!" exclaimed Brogan.

"Why the hell should anyone want to pray for me?"

"Just because you do not pray for yourself and probably not even for others is no reason why others should not pray for you. These are good, simple people."

"Sorry, Padre," apologised Brogan, "I didn't mean to sound bitter or anythin', it's just that I ain't used to that kind of thing."

The young woman appeared beside them bearing a large bowl which she placed alongside Brogan. He looked at it suspiciously and even more suspiciously at the bar of soap the woman produced from her pocket.

"Is that real soap?" he demanded.

"Of course, *señor*," she smiled. "Soap is necessary if you are to be washed properly."

"Washed properly!" he exclaimed. "Ma'am, I'll have you know that it just ain't natural for a body to be washed with real soap, it goes against nature."

The woman might have been quite young but she seemed to know her own mind and was very firm. "Is it natural to be always dirty?" she smiled. "Your body needs to be washed to allow it to breathe properly."

The priest intervened. "Besides, Señor Brogan, you have been badly burned and if you are not washed there is great danger that disease will complete the task where the tin hut failed."

Brogan's fingers touched his burned arm and he winced slightly. He realized that his dislike of soap and water would have to be suppressed in the interests of his future health. He drank the remainder of his coffee, tasted the soup and decided that he did not like it as it was far too spicy for his taste but took a bite out of the piece of bread which was hard and stale but he forced it down. He sighed heavily and spread his arms. "Do your damnedest, woman!" he invited.

* * *

It had not actually been a bath, but it had been the next best thing in that he was stripped totally naked and washed all over despite his objections that it was only his chest, arms and head that were really burnt. The woman, who was named Anna, did not seem in the slightest way embarrassed at seeing a naked man, although she was not married.

"What chance does a girl have to get married?" she smiled. "All the young men have either been drafted into the army or have fled to the hills. Besides . . . " she blushed slightly, "I am no longer a virgin and most men do not like it if their bride is not a virgin. *Si*, I have been taken by the soldiers . . . more than once."

"Sorry 'bout that," said Brogan more for something to say than from any conviction.

"Why should you be sorry?" she smiled. "It is not you who has been robbed of your virginity."

It was Padre Miguel who was the

more embarrassed of the three and coughed his disapproval of the line the conversation was taking. Anna looked up at him, smiled and apologized.

Rather to Brogan's dismay, his clothes were gathered up and carried from the church by Anna who laughingly announced that they too were to be thoroughly washed. Padre Miguel produced a spare brown habit which was far too small for Brogan but at least it did cover certain vital parts.

"You must remain here," said the padre. "Tomorrow Colonel Sanchez returns and it would be better if he believes that you are too ill to be questioned."

"And Lieutenant Granta?" asked Brogan.

"Him also," replied the priest. "He may be a good man in many ways but he is still a soldier and must obey orders. I do not think he would do anything more to you, but if Colonel Sanchez orders it then he is bound to obey. As well as being a good man, he is also a very good soldier. Perhaps one day he will become powerful in the army and be able to issue his own orders."

"If the system hasn't got the better of him by then," said Brogan.

Padre Miguel nodded sagely. "*Si*, the system. You are right, nobody beats the system but they may be able to help form the direction that system takes."

4

LIEUTENANT GRANTA stood over Brogan and smiled. "The robes of a priest do not become you, Mr McNally," he said. "Padre Miguel said that you were too ill for anyone to talk to but I am sorry to say that I did not believe him."

"I sure ain't ready to leap over no fences," said Brogan from his position on the rough palliasse that had been provided for him.

"I can see that," smiled the lieutenant. "It is perhaps very fortunate for you that Colonel Sanchez did not give any instructions as to how long you had to remain in the hut. Had he done so you would probably not be alive now."

"You would have left me there even though he isn't here?"

"Of course," nodded the lieutenant, "it would have been an order and I do not disobey any orders."

"Even if you don't agree with 'em?"

"Even then," came the bland reply. "I have had to carry out a good many orders with which I do not agree, but I am a soldier, Mr McNally, I do not have the luxury you have in deciding what to do."

"I guess not," conceded Brogan. "Maybe that's why I chose the life of a saddletramp, just so's I wouldn't have to obey no orders I didn't agree with."

"Each life has its advantages and disadvantages," grinned the lieutenant. "However, I do not come just to see how you are, although I am pleased to see you in such good health after your ordeal. I come to tell you that before he left, Colonel Sanchez gave the order that should you survive, which he doubted, you were to be held until he returned. It would appear that he has a use for you."

"Is that good or bad?" grinned Brogan.

"It is good in that it probably means that you will remain alive, for the time being at least, but I must confess that is hardly ever good news when he decides that someone has their uses."

"I guess that means he wants me to do his dirty work for him," said Brogan. "It usually does. I'll take a wager with you that he wants to use me to get close to Hemenez."

Lieutenant Granta laughed. "You are indeed a very astute man, Mr McNally He has not said so but that is what I believe as well."

"I could tell him to go to hell."

"Which is where you would find yourself a few seconds after telling him," smiled the lieutenant. "I have seen others attempt to defy him and always they have been shot either by him or by one of his bodyguard who go everywhere with him."

"Well why did he order me into that hut?" asked Brogan. "I could've died an' been no use at all to him."

Granta shrugged. "It is of little

consequence to him one way or the other. If you die that is the end of the matter and if you live then he will make use of you."

"So he wants to use me," mused Brogan. "Does that mean you're goin' to lock me up somewhere else?"

The lieutenant smiled. "I do not believe that will be necessary. I have been observing that a certain young lady by the name of Anna has been tending you. She is a very attractive young woman. She is to be your prison, Mr McNally; should you try to escape she will be taken and subjected to a most painful death, after the soldiers have had their way with her of course. I once witnessed a young woman subjected to rape by over thirty men, one after the other. She died of course. Even if she does not die during such an ordeal her subsequent death will be very slow and most painful."

Brogan looked at Lieutenant Luis Del Marco Granta in a very new light. "You're just as big a bastard as any of

81

'em!" he growled.

The lieutenant simply laughed. "I am a soldier, Mr McNally, a very good soldier and a very ambitious one."

★ ★ ★

Brogan told both Anna and Padre Miguel what had been said and while the padre did show some surprise, Anna simply shrugged.

"He is a soldier, as he says, and it is to be expected," she said. "Do not have any thought for me, Señor Brogan. I am nobody, I am no concern of yours. If you should decide to escape I shall not hold anything against you."

"Anna is right," said Padre Miguel, sadly. "We cannot expect such as you to have any great concern for the likes of us. Should you choose to escape I will willingly help you and I am sure Anna will as well." Anna nodded.

Brogan sighed heavily. "I ain't sure if you meant it or not, Padre, but you just made it almost impossible for me to leave. I ain't like that. Most folk can look after themselves and I wouldn't raise a finger to help but I couldn't ride out knowin' I'd just condemned an innocent person to death."

★ ★ ★

The turn of events weighed heavily on his mind that night and he cursed Lieutenant Granta and decided that he was even more dangerous than Colonel Sanchez. At least with Sanchez the demarcation lines were very clear and he did not seem devious enough to think of something like Granta had. As far as Brogan knew he had never had any dealings with Englishmen, although he had come across one or two and he decided that it must be his English upbringing which had made Granta as devious as he seemed.

However, his ordeal had also taken a heavy toll on his body and before long he was asleep, although he did dream, a very confused dream.

Anna brought his clothes back early the following morning and Brogan had to confess to her enquiry as to whether the wash had done him any harm, that it had not and that he felt the better for it.

"That don't mean I'm goin' to make a habit of it though," he objected. "I'll go along with it this time just 'cos it was necessary for my health. Normally all over bathin' with real soap ain't no good to no man."

Anna laughed. "You sound just like my little brother used to sound. He too did not like the feel of water and would do anything to avoid a bath, but then I think all small boys are the same. Are you a small boy, Señor Brogan?"

"I guess you could answer that question yourself," grinned Brogan. "There ain't too many women who've seen me stripped."

"I suspect the last one being your mother!" she laughed. "Now, let me look at your arms, they are the most badly burned. I have here a salve which my mother uses for such things." She laughed again. "My mother, she is very old fashioned. She knows that I have seen your naked body and already she is making noises that if I am not to be classed as a whore I must marry you."

"Marry me!" grinned Brogan. "I'm probably older'n your mother."

"She knows this," shrugged Anna as she applied some of the salve to Brogan's reddened skin. "I too know this. Such things are not important."

"What about the soldiers you say took you," said Brogan, "were you expected to marry one of them too?"

"That is different," she smiled as she rubbed in the salve. "Then I was taken by force, as was my mother also. As I say, my mother she is very old fashioned and to her even tending to the injuries of a single man and especially washing his body is something that no unattached woman should do. Such things must always be undertaken by married women only." She laughed. "It seems that the naked body of a man is something that must remain a mystery until a woman is married."

"Well you can tell your mother that I must disappoint her, this is one *gringo* hombre who ain't ready to get himself hitched to no woman, no matter how good lookin' that woman may be an' you sure are a fine-lookin' woman."

Anna laughed and applied some more salve and rubbed a little too hard for Brogan's comfort. He tried not to wince but failed.

"I have already told her this," she said. "As I have already told her that since you are an American *gringo* and plainly far too old that it can never be."

"So you'll have to settle for some ancient peon old enough to be your grandfather?"

"If necessary, *Si*," she smiled. "Age is not important."

"But you just said I was too old," objected Brogan.

"*Si*, an old *gringo*!" she laughed and roughly turned him on to his front and proceeded to apply the salve to his back.

★ ★ ★

That evening Brogan was given a simple meal but he sensed that even such a meal meant that someone else must go hungry. Padre Miguel had told him that the soldiers had commandeered almost all the food in the town, as was their normal habit.

"Usually they come for twenty-four hours only and everyone is prepared for such a thing," said the padre. "This time however, they come for at least three days. Already most of the food is gone and they are demanding more. They do not believe us when we say we do not have any more. They are convinced that we have secret stores somewhere."

"And do you?" asked Brogan.

The priest had not replied, simply smiled.

Even though he felt a little guilty at eating the meal, he realized that these people would be far too proud to admit that anyone was going without as a result, so he ate it and, bland and simple as it was, he felt the better for it.

Later, Anna returned and rubbed more salve into his aching body and he felt that it was beginning to have some effect. Already there seemed to be less heat in his flesh and his joints now moved a little more freely. Later still, Lieutenant Granta made a brief appearance but said little other than to confirm that his superior should be back in the town sometime during the following morning. Apart from the distant barking of a dog, silence fell upon the town and Brogan soon succumbed to sleep.

★ ★ ★

The clump of heavy boots and shouts of "Gringo" echoing around the church made Brogan sit up, somewhat painfully as two soldiers appeared from either side of the altar, behind which he had slept, and pointed their rifles threateningly.

Their message was quite clear, even spoken as it was in Spanish and Brogan slowly struggled to his feet. He was pushed roughly towards the door where he blinked at the bright sun for a moment and was very surprised to note that it was well up in the sky which meant that it was probably about ten o'clock. Normally he would have been awake at dawn but his ordeal had obviously taken its toll.

Once again he was prodded roughly and forced across the square towards the cantina where, stopping at the water trough, he tried to take a drink. One of his guards laughed, placed his hand on Brogan's neck as he lowered his head to drink and forced his head into the water where he attempted to hold it under. However, weakened as he was, Brogan was still too powerful for the rather diminutive soldier and for a moment both men stared hatred at each other, the soldier fingering his rifle suggestively.

The situation was saved by an order barked by a sergeant and the two guards sullenly withdrew.

"I must apologize for the behaviour of my men," rasped the sergeant gutturally. "Please, Señor, you must be thirsty, drink what you will, I am sure the horses will not mind." He laughed at what he thought was a joke.

Brogan gave the sergeant what he hoped was a withering stare and quite deliberately lowered his head and drank some more. When he looked up Lieutenant Granta was standing in the doorway of the cantina smiling.

"You are either a very brave or a very foolish man, Mr McNally," said Granta. "There are few who would dare do even what you have just done."

Brogan wiped his mouth on his sleeve, deliberately spat on to the ground and wiped his sleeve across his mouth once again.

"But then I ain't one of your downtrodden peons," he said eventually "I come from a free country."

The lieutenant grinned and stepped aside, giving an exaggerated bow and sweeping his arm to wave Brogan into the cantina. "Then perhaps it would have been better for you had you remained in America, although I am not too certain that you have all that many more freedoms than these peons. However, that is a matter for debate and we do not have the time."

The cantina had obviously been transformed into an office for the military. Two desks had appeared from somewhere, one for the sergeant and the other for Lieutenant Granta. Granta indicated that Brogan should stand in front of the desk as he went to sit down.

"I have a message from Colonel Sanchez," explaind the lieutenant. "He has unfortunately been delayed for a few hours. However, I am authorized to make you an offer, Mr McNally, and I am quite certain that it is an offer you cannot refuse."

Brogan laughed. "I guess that don't need any explainin'. I accept whatever it is you want me to do or I'm stood against a wall and shot."

Granta smiled and nodded. "Something like that. I must confess that it makes a pleasant change to talk to a man who understands. You were quite right when you said Colonel Snachez wanted to use you to get close to Hemenez. That is the deal, Mr McNally. Since you plainly have a certain amount of influence with Hemenez and he is probably the most wanted criminal in this part of Mexico, it can only be to our mutual benefit if you work with us in apprehending this dangerous criminal."

"I'm beginnin' to wonder who's

the criminal, Hemenez or the army," replied Brogan.

"Such things are not for you to wonder about," smiled Granta although his eyes told Brogan that here was a very ruthless man. "In Mexico the army is the law and therefore cannot be criminals."

"I guess they ain't none of my business," sighed Brogan. "So exactly what do you want me to do?"

The lieutenant looked somewhat surprised. "You give in very easily, Mr McNally. I must admit to a feeling of disappointment, I had expected you to argue."

"I never said I was agreein'," said Brogan. "All I asked was what I was supposed to do to earn my life."

"That's better!" laughed the lieutenant. "It is just as I said, you must use your influence with Hemenez to lure him into a trap. Exactly how you do it is obviously a matter entirely for you."

"And if I refuse I'm shot," said Brogan.

"Of course," nodded Granta. "But first you will be forced to witness the rape and torture of the woman called Anna and possibly even the torture and execution of Padre Miguel."

"I was right," snarled Brogan. "You are a bigger bastard than Sanchez. He ain't devious enough to think of somethin' like that."

The lieutenant smiled and nodded. "I shall take that as a compliment, Mr McNally. It is true, Colonel Sanchez lacks imagination, but he is a good soldier for all that."

Brogan gave a sardonic laugh. "I thought all soldiers, American as well as Mexican, had all imagination removed from their bodies the day they enlisted."

"A few of us are allowed to keep it intact," countered Granta. "I also consider myself to be a student of human nature, which is why I did not lock you away last night. I knew that you would not risk the life of the woman, just as I know that you will not risk her life again, just as you will not risk that of Padre Miguel."

"I guess the padre wouldn't be too bothered, he'd just be meetin' his Maker a mite sooner'n he thought he would."

"Possibly so," nodded Granta. "Although I have never yet met a priest who is not afraid of death."

"Why the padre?" asked Brogan. "Surely you wouldn't kill him, let alone torture him. I hear the Church is pretty powerful in Mexico, they wouldn't stand for it."

"Even they could not prevent such a thing if it were proved that he was helping the *bandidos* and refusing aid to the military."

"Meanin' what?"

"Meaning that we know the padre is hoarding food and quite a lot of other things, just as we know his sympathies are with the *bandidos*. He claims that he knows nothing about hoarding food. For a priest to tell lies is not good."

"Well I sure ain't seen much sign of food," said Brogan, "what they've given me is hardly fit for pigs to eat."

"They are used to living like pigs," smiled the lieutenant. "What do you say, Mr McNally, do you agree to help us bring the *bandido* Hemenez to justice?"

"Can't say as I agree with your idea of justice," said Brogan, "but I will agree that you have a very persuasive way of putting things."

"Your life and the woman's!" laughed Granta. "Your problem is, Mr McNally, that you are too noble."

"That remains to be seen," grinned Brogan.

* * *

Nothing much happened for the remainder of the morning, other than Brogan told Anna and Padre Miguel what had happened and once again they both urged him to forget about them and save himself.

"Even if you do help them capture Hemenez," the padre pointed out, "I know the way the mind of the Mexican military works. Once they have made use of you, you will be shot and there will be nobody to deny whatever story they care to tell."

"I know that," said Brogan, "and I think Lieutenant Granta knows I know it. Don't you worry none about me, I've been in sticky situations before and am still alive to tell the tale."

"There will come a day when you will not be," reminded Anna.

"Then my worries will be over," said Brogan.

Their conversation was interrupted by the arrival, through the pass, of a troop of soldiers who were followed a short while later by a rather grand carriage out of which stepped Colonel Sanchez and another, well dressed and obviously very important, man whom Brogan took to be the minister.

A hurried conversation took place between Colonel Sanchez and Lieutenant Granta whilst the minister strutted about the square displaying his finery and importance, although it was plain that the few townspeople who were there were far from impressed and had the minister seen several small children also strutting about mimicking him, he would not have been very pleased. To his credit, Lieutenant Granta, who did see the children, simply smiled and ignored them. The lieutenant had plainly been given some instructions since he hurried off to organize his men. A few minutes later the reason became obvious.

A group of about thirty peons suddenly appeared, mostly men but there were about five or six women, all roped together and with ankles hobbled. They were all roughly herded into the centre of the square and forced to stand in ragged and sorrowful rows in the burning heat of the afternoon sun. They were left standing for almost an hour under the sneering and taunting eyes of a few guards lounging in the shade. Colonel Sanchez and the minister entered the priest's house and a short while later food was carried in to them.

After they had eaten, the colonel and the minister appeared at the doorway and a command was barked out to Lieutenant Granta who in turn repeated the order to his men. The soldiers immediately dispersed around the town and slowly returned herding frightened women and children and a few old men before them. They too were forced to stand in the square, facing the other peons. Padre Miguel was allowed to stand alongside Brogan.

"What's goin' on?" asked Brogan.

"I fear you are about to witness an execution," replied the priest, sadly. "In fact I fear that you are about to witness a great number of executions."

"Executions!" exclaimed Brogan. "What for?"

"It is claimed that these people have been helping the *bandidos*, and it is also claimed that they have been involved in attacks upon the military."

"And have they?"

The padre shrugged. "It is possible, *Si*, I cannot say for certain, but I think most unlikely. I know these people, they are from a village not far away, up in the mountains. As here, it is more than likely that many of their menfolk have fled to the hills and have joined the *bandidos*, but not these people. As you can see, the men are almost all very old, too old to join the resistance in body, although their minds joined them long ago."

"And they're goin' to be shot?"

The padre nodded gravely. "It seems so."

"Why bring them here?"

"As a warning to others," sighed the padre. "There is nobody left in their village now. It would be pointless to execute them where nobody else could witness it. It is to remind the people of Santa Cruz what will happen to them if they refuse to co-operate."

Colonel Sanchez nodded to Lieutenant Granta who stepped forward and addressed the hapless villagers. Padre

Miguel translated for Brogan's benefit as he spoke, although the gist of it was more or less exactly as he had explained to Brogan. When he had finished, Lieutenant Granta invited the head man to step forward and explain himself on behalf of the villagers.

There was little the old man could say other than to deny that they had either given succour and sustenance to the *bandidos* voluntarily but that what help they had given had been forced upon them under threat of death. He also denied that any of the villagers had ever taken part in attacks upon the military. When he had finished he stepped back into line, head bowed.

Colonel Sanchez now took up position alongside Lieutenant Granta and addressed the villagers and again Padre Miguel translated.

Although he used flowery language, the main point of what he said was that the villagers had been found guilty of serious crimes against the military and there was only one punishment that could be given, that of death by firing squad. For the first time there was some reaction amongst them, although it was confined to a few words passing between themselves and a few glances around.

"No children!" Brogan hissed to Padre Miguel. "I thought there was somethin' wrong but I couldn't think what it was until now. There's no children. Surely there must be some children!"

Padre Miguel looked sadly up at Brogan and shook his head. "You are quite right, *señor*, there are no children."

Brogan stared at the padre, uncertain if he understood correctly or not.

"Dead?" he asked.

"*Si*, all dead!" replied Padre Miguel.

5

BROGAN suddenly stepped forward and was immediately met with almost every soldier raising their guns to their shoulders. He raised his arms to indicate that he was unarmed and moved closer to Colonel Sanchez who, although knowing that Brogan was unarmed, shrank back in apparent fear.

"I'll do a deal with you, Colonel," said Brogan. "You spare these people an' I'll help you catch Hemenez."

By this time two soldiers had rushed to Brogan and had seized his arms, bending them roughly and painfully behind his back.

Seeing that he was now held securely, Colonel Sanchez recovered his composure and moved towards Brogan. "I do not think that you are in any position to make deals, *gringo*. It is quite within my power to have you executed along with these other criminals."

"Criminals!" said Brogan, defiantly. "Old men and women, that's all they are an' you know it."

"Criminals!" exploded Sanchez. "And like all criminals they will meet their just end."

"Hemenez," reminded Brogan, "he trusts me. You need me to get close to him. You free these people an' I'll help you catch him."

Lieutenant Granta whispered in the colonel's ear, although he need not have done since Brogan did not understand Spanish. When he had listened Sanchez smiled and an order was barked at the two men holding Brogan and he was dragged back to stand alongside the padre with the two soldiers still holding him.

Another order was given by Lieutenant Granta and five men and one woman were dragged from the ragged lines of peons, the ropes tying them to the others cut and they were led away to stand alongside the church where six soldiers, under the command of Lieutenant Granta's sergeant had already taken up position.

There was no doubting what was about to happen and all Brogan could do was watch in fascinated horror and listen to the steady intonations of Padre Miguel as he fingered his rosary praying for the unfortunate victims.

For a brief moment there was a futile show of defiance as the five shouted in praise of Pablo Hemenez and they stood erect, heads raised, awaiting their fate.

The end came swiftly: a volley of shots and all fell to the ground and the sergeant moved forward carrying a pistol and examined each body. His pistol fired twice into the heads of two who had not died.

Almost immediately six more victims were pushed forward and made to stand against the wall, even having to step over the bodies of their companions. Once again the soldiers raised their rifles and once again six bodies fell with only one needing to be despatched by the sergeant. The operation was repeated three more times until all the villagers had been executed.

During this slaughter, both Colonel Sanchez and the minister had withdrawn to Padre Miguel's house, the minister plainly fighting to control the contents of his stomach. Colonel Sanchez on the other hand seemed almost reluctant to miss a thing but he knew his priorities lay with the minister. When the executions had ended, Colonel Sanchez reappeared and ordered that Brogan be brought over to him.

"Now, *gringo*," smirked the colonel. "What was that you said about a deal?"

"You just played all your aces," growled Brogan.

"You think so?" smiled the colonel. "What you have just witnessed was the just fate of any criminal. They were all criminals, Señor McNally, just as all the people of Santa Cruz are criminals. If you wish, I can order the execution of every man, woman and child in Santa Cruz."

"And what good would that do you?" asked Brogan. "You can't kill every peon in the territory."

"Do not taunt me!" snapped Sanchez. "I can order the death of anyone I wish. I could wipe out the entire population of this territory should I wish."

"Then you'd have nobody left to govern," Brogan pointed out.

"And I would have no trouble," sneered Sanchez. "However, much more important as far as you are concerned, Señor McNally, I can order that you be executed. Is that what you want? Are you so very keen to meet your God?"

"Don't know if He'd be too keen on meetin' me," smiled Brogan. "I guess I got my place booked down below stokin' up them hell fires. If I get there before you I'll keep you a good place."

"Do not try to be funny or clever with me," snapped the colonel. He nodded to Lieutenant Granta who spoke to one of his men. The man raced away and a short while later both Anna and Padre Miguel were pushed through the tangle of bodies now strewn alongside the church and made to stand against the wall.

"Do I give the order for my men to shoot?" asked Granta.

Colonel Sanchez laughed. "Only Señor McNally can give that order," he said. "If he agrees to help capture Hemenez, then they go free, for the moment at least. If he refuses to help then they die where they are."

"Señor McNally?" asked Granta, inclining his head and smiling. "Your orders if you please."

Brogan had a hard time preventing himself from lashing out at the two officers but he managed to control his urges and after a long stare of hatred at both men he finally nodded. "I guess I ain't got no choice. OK, let 'em go.

You have my word I'll find Hemenez for you."

"Such a sensible decision," beamed Colonel Sanchez. "I leave the details up to you, Lieutenant. Now I must see to our guest. It would seem that he is unused to witnessing executions."

"We shall discuss the details in the cantina," smiled Granta. "But first I have other things to do."

"Like get rid of them bodies?" grunted Brogan. "Was that really necessary?"

"I am afraid so," grinned the lieutenant. "However, it is not up to me to clear the bodies. That will be done by the peons of Santa Cruz. I shall speak to you later, Mr McNally."

Brogan went across to where Anna and Padre Miguel still stood against the wall and picked his way through the bodies around which vast numbers of flies were already gathering.

"Why did you agree?" demanded Anna almost as if she had in some way been betrayed.

"Because I had to," replied Brogan. "Sure, I could've let 'em shoot you an' the padre an' then someone else an' someone else until there was only me left an' if I hadn't agreed then I'd've been killed too."

"He is right," soothed Padre Miguel looking around sadly at the carnage at his feet. "Come, we must bury these poor souls as quickly as possible." He looked up at the sky. "See, already the vultures gather, they sense a meal."

Brogan had already seen the large birds slowly circling the town, birds which sensed death almost before it happened. The padre summoned the other townsfolk and soon several of the more able men, including Brogan, were hard at work digging into the baked earth.

There were no individual graves, even though some of the victims were related to townsfolk and when all thirty bodies were laid in the grave, each shrouded in a white winding sheet, Padre Miguel conducted a brief but moving service. Then the mass grave was filled in under the sneering gaze of some of the soldiers. There were suggestions from some of the more uncouth soldiers that it might be a good thing if the others were to join their compatriots.

"Only six women," observed Brogan as the final shovel of earth was scattered over the bodies. "I would have expected more."

"No children and only the old women," observed Padre Miguel. "The younger women, I fear they suffered much before they died." He sighed and looked up at the birds still circling. "There is no meal for them here but where these poor souls have come from I fear there is much to eat."

★ ★ ★

Later, Brogan was summoned before Colonel Sanchez who looked the saddletramp up and down disdainfully "A noble but futile gesture on your part,

Señor McNally," he said. "As you see, I have the power of life and death over these people — and you."

"Was it really necessary?" asked Brogan. "Old men and old women, what possible threat could they be to you?"

Colonel Sanchez laughed. "Threat! Who talks of threat? Examples needed to be made. It is unfortunate but it also a fact of life. You are wise to agree to help us capture the criminal Hemenez; had you not done so your body would now be among those buried."

"If you say so," nodded Brogan, biting on his tongue to prevent him saying what he really felt.

"*Si*, I say so," grinned the colonel. "Lieutenant Granta will give you your orders, orders I warn you not to disobey. Even should you manage to escape to America, think of what you leave behind, the price of your freedom."

"The woman, Anna, and Padre Miguel," observed Brogan.

"Among others," nodded Sanchez. He waved his hand to dismiss Brogan and turned his attention to other matters. Brogan did not argue and turned and walked out into the square.

Lieutenant Granta was crossing the square but stopped and waited for Brogan to approach him. The two men stared an understanding hatred at each other for a moment before Granta laughed.

"You would like to kill me, Mr McNally! I can understand that but it does not matter. Come, we have matters to discuss." He turned sharply on his heels and marched back towards the cantina.

The coolness of the cantina was most welcome after having toiled in the heat of the sun and, rather surprisingly, the lieutenant offered Brogan a glass of lemonade.

"What's to discuss?" asked Brogan as he accepted the lemonade.

"What's to discuss?" mimicked Granta. "There is indeed much to discuss, Mr

McNally. Please take a seat . . . " He indicated a nearby chair. Brogan did think about refusing but realized it would be a futile gesture and sat. "I am a military man," Granta continued, "as you well know and I believe you know enough of the military mind to know that even I need to operate within certain rules. I have to have plans, plans of campaign and plans of what to do should things go wrong or not work out quite as they should."

"I hardly ever make plans," said Brogan, "they usually do go wrong."

"That all depends upon who makes those plans," smiled Granta.

"My plans very rarely go wrong, but I am always prepared. Now, I have information that Hemenez is in the hills to the north-west of here, in American terms, about twenty miles. It is a wild area, no villages, not even the odd farm. Frankly it would be impossible for an army patrol to approach without being seen and there are too many places where we could be easily ambushed."

"So what do you expect me to do," smiled Brogan, "take 'em all on single handed?"

Granta laughed. "If such a thing were possible, why not? However, I very much doubt that it will be possible. You are to infiltrate them and somehow persuade Hemenez to leave his stronghold and travel through a valley along which flows the Rio Negro, Hemenez will know it well."

"And just how the hell do I do that?" asked Brogan. "I can't see Hemenez takin' much notice of me."

The lieutenant laughed. "Very true, in fact he is more likely to kill you before you have a chance of doing anything but we must suppose that he does not kill you . . . "

"The more I hear the less I like the odds," said Brogan.

"And you prefer the odds if you should refuse?"

"I guess I'll take my chance with Hemenez," nodded Brogan.

"I thought you would," smiled Granta. "Now, I know that Hemenez and his followers are desperate for money, even rebels such as he must have money, he cannot steal everything . . . "

"The army seem to," said Brogan.

The lieutenant stiffened slightly. "Some elements might, but not my unit. My men are professionals, the best. I do not tolerate stealing. It is true we take what food we need, but nothing else. They are not allowed to loot. I personally shoot anyone found guilty of such things."

"And rape?" queried Brogan.

Granta shrugged. "They are only men, they do not kill the women. We digress, Mr McNally. You are to tell Hemenez that you have overheard a conversation between myself and Colonel Sanchez concerning the transportation of money from here to the military garrison at Ciudad Juarez on the border. He will not be surprised, money and gold is often sent there, and from here the route is along the Rio Negro."

"And are you?" asked Brogan.

The lieutenant smiled. "As a matter of fact it is true, but that is not important. What is important is that Hemenez believes you."

Brogan was not too certain if the claim that money was actually to be transported was for his benefit or not but he was willing to believe that it was and that Granta was prepared to risk the money in order to capture Hemenez.

"When?"

"In four days' time," said Granta. "We leave here early in the morning and expect to be in the valley of the Rio Negro during that afternoon. Of course my men will be positioned in the valley in advance. The gold is to be transported by soldiers directly responsible to Colonel Sanchez."

"I hope he knows you're riskin' his money," laughed Brogan.

Lieutenant Granta smiled. "I do not tell the colonel everything. There are things it is better even he, as military governor, should not get to know."

"Four days," said Brogan. "That don't give me much time. Can't you delay it a couple of days?"

"Impossible," replied Granta firmly "The matter is out of my hands. You must leave here at first light in the morning . . . " He grinned knowingly. "That will give you one night to seek solace in the arms of Anna."

"That's somethin' I can do without any time," said Brogan. "OK, I don't suppose I've got much choice. What about my horse and guns?"

"They will be made available to you in the morning," smiled Granta. "You will have no need of them before." He laughed. "Are you sure that that old horse of yours will make the journey?"

"Me an' her have been through a lot together an' she ain't never let me down yet."

"There are better horses available in the town," said Granta.

"An' just what do you reckon Hemenez'll think if he sees me on a strange horse? I thought you were an intelligent man, Lieutenant."

The lieutenant nodded and smiled. "Of course, you are quite right, it is better if all seems normal. I shall give you further instructions in the morning."

★ ★ ★

Colonel Sanchez and the minister left Santa Cruz about an hour later, both riding in the comfort of the minister's coach and accompanied by a troop of about forty outriders. With their departure a slightly more relaxed atmosphere descended upon the town with Lieutenant Granta's men plainly under orders not to antagonize the townsfolk in any way.

Brogan told Anna and Padre Miguel what his orders were and once again he was urged to take the opportunity to make good his own escape and he told them that he would give it serious consideration, although he knew that he would go through with it.

With the departure of Colonel Sanchez and the minister, good quality food suddenly appeared and some was even given to Granta and his men, albeit grudgingly. The lieutenant did not question where the food had come from although he did pass a comment to Padre Miguel about 'God working in mysterious ways'.

Brogan was moved out of the church and into the padre's house and after a filling but slightly too spicy meal for his taste, Brogan spent an hour grooming and talking to his horse. There was nothing unusual in this, he often talked to her and was firmly convinced that she understood his every word and was even capable of giving her opinions on certain matters.

"Do you think we ought to hightail it as soon as we can?" he asked her. She nodded her head vigorously "You would," Brogan continued. "Anythin' for an easy life, that's you. Well I got news for you, old girl, we is goin' through with it for the sake of Anna and the padre if nothin' else."

"You are indeed a very strange and unusual man, *señor*," a voice said behind him.

"Must be losin' my grip," replied Brogan not bothering to turn. "I can normally hear a fly land on a piece of shit from a hundred yards but I sure didn't hear you."

"I can move quieter than the cat does when stalking a mouse or a bird," said Anna coming to his side. "I think you did not hear me because you were too busy talking to your horse. Does she agree with what you are doing?"

"Nope, but then she hardly ever does," grinned Brogan.

"Then this time listen to what she has to say," smiled Anna. "If she says you must save yourself, so be it."

"You seem mighty anxious to die," observed Brogan.

"We all must die sometime," she smiled, stroking the neck of the horse. "Even a man like you."

"I try to put it off whenever I can," grinned Brogan. "So far I've succeeded pretty well. I'm gettin' old though, if a bullet don't get me it can't be too long before old Father Time decides I've been around long enough. You're young though, you got a good many years ahead of you."

"God willing," she smiled.

"I wouldn't rely too much on Him," said Brogan. "It seems to me that Lieutenant Granta's got more control over that side of things than any god."

"Even he must answer to the Lord," said Anna.

"If'n you say so," sighed Brogan. "It's what he does in the meantime what worries me."

"I understand what you mean, *señor*," she demurred. "Of course you are right." She touched his arm and smiled weakly. "If you wish it, I am yours. It is the least I can do in return for what you do for me and Padre Miguel."

Brogan was not prone to blushing and indeed it was very difficult to tell if he was or not with his weather-beaten features but he knew that he had. "I thank you kindly ma'am," he said quietly, "but that won't be necessary. 'Sides, I don't want that mother of yours chasin' me with no shotgun forcin' me to wed you."

Anna laughed gently. "You do not find me attractive enough to marry?" she asked.

"Hell, it ain't that," said Brogan, slightly flustered. "You is one hell of a fine woman, it's just that I ain't the marryin' kind as you'd soon find out. I couldn't settle down, I need to wander."

"My mother need never know anything," she smiled.

Brogan was beginning to feel very uncomfortable, he always did in such situations and was never quite sure how to handle it.

"Ma'am," he said quietly, "it ain't that I ain't never had me a woman before, I've had my share, 'specially when I was younger, it's just that . . . well . . . I'm old enough to be your grandfather."

"But you're not," she smiled disarmingly "I will not press you, *señor*, but should you change your mind my house is two doors from the cantina and I live alone. My mother, she lives at the far side of town, she need never know anything."

Brogan felt himself blush again. "I'll have to think about it," he said, "but don't hold out no hopes."

She laughed. "You are indeed a strange man, Señor McNally I never before have met a man who would refuse the chance to bed with a younger woman."

"Well you have now," said Brogan. "Hell, you'll soon forget all about me or come to realize that I just ain't worth the bother. I leave in the mornin' an' I reckon that'll be the last time you'll ever see me. It could be that I succeed in trappin' Hemenez but it could also be that I get myself killed either in the process or never get that far. Even if I don't it'll be most unlikely I'll ever be this way again."

She smiled and suddenly reached up to give him a kiss on his cheek. "All will be well, I feel it. As for the other thing, it is a pity. Good men are hard to find these days."

"Who said I was a good man?"

"I do and Padre Miguel says so too. You may be a man who is prepared to fight and kill and have probably killed many times, but that does not make you a bad man. It cannot be so or you would not hesitate to escape and leave us to our fate without a thought."

"I ain't rode out of town yet," he reminded.

She laughed. "Listen to your horse, she has more sense than you." She turned and went to the door of the small stable. "Remember what I said, *señor*, I am yours should you wish it. Two doors from the cantina."

6

BROGAN rode out of Santa Cruz shortly after dawn, armed with instructions on how to find the Rio Negro and roughly where Pablo Hemenez was thought to be. He had not seen Anna but could sense that she watched him leave, as did most of the other citizens.

Finding the valley of the Rio Negro proved easy enough and he followed the river upstream, reaching the head of the valley at mid-afternoon, having stopped twice to rest and water his horse. The head of the valley opened out into a flat, treeless plain which appeared to be about seven or eight miles wide before it gave way to towering mountains. It was somewhere in these mountains that Hemenez was supposed to be hiding.

The feeling that his progress was being watched had been with Brogan for some time and the feeling increased as he began the ascent of the mountains and more than once he caught a glimpse of movement among the rocks which he chose to pretend he had not seen. Had anyone been intent on killing him there had been plenty of opportunities so he assumed that it was either curiosity or they were under instruction from Hemenez not to attempt anything.

Once off the plain, there was little choice of trails, the one he was on seeming to be the only one. Certainly any other route would have meant trying to negotiate masses of rocks and sheer cliffs and he could see why the army chose not to hunt Hemenez; a handful of men could easily hold off an entire regiment.

★ ★ ★

Rather to his surprise, there was no challenge to his progress for almost an hour and Brogan was beginning to believe that Hemenez was prepared

127

to let him pass unhindered which presented him with the problem of whether or not he should just continue and forget all about Anna, Padre Miguel and Santa Cruz.

Logic told him to just keep riding but his instinct rebelled against the thought of what might happen in Santa Cruz. However, his concern turned to something akin to relief as he rounded a bend and was faced with three Mexicans, their guns aimed steadily at him.

"Wondered when the hell you was goin' to do somethin'," said Brogan. The men looked at him a little uncomprehendingly and he realized that they probably did not speak English. "Hemenez," he said. "Pablo Hemenez!"

"*Si*, Hemenez," said one of the men, indicating that Brogan should get off his horse. Brogan looked about, realized that the three men did not have any horses, sighed and dismounted.

Once he was off his horse, the three

men seemed a little happier and the one who had spoken waved his gun indicating a small track to his left, turned and marched off along it. The other two waited for Brogan to lead his horse ahead of them before closing in behind, their rifles still at the ready.

The narrow track rose steeply, twisting and turning among the rocks, making it obvious as to why they had not used horses — riding would have been impossible. Eventually they reached the top of the escarpment and the track straightened up and slightly downwards towards a small, clear lake. They followed the edge of the lake before climbing again. This time the climb was short and ended abruptly at a group of rough, stone houses, all thatched with earth. It was from the first of these that a familiar figure emerged.

"Welcome!" grinned Pablo Hemenez. "I wondered if we should meet again, *gringo*."

"I was beginnin' to wonder myself," said Brogan, releasing his horse into the hands of a youth who led it through to a small corral behind the huts. "You ought to give your men lessons in keepin' someone under observation without bein' seen."

Hemenez laughed. "They are but ignorant peons more used to farming than the life of a *bandido*. Come, *gringo*, I have questions to ask you." He led the way into the hut where he offered Brogan a rough looking cheroot which was refused. "I sense that you do not come this way by chance, *gringo*, I think you have been sent by Sanchez."

"It sure ain't my choice, that's for certain," admitted Brogan seating himself on a large rock which appeared to serve as a seat in the absence of any other furniture. "I don't know about Sanchez, this was all Lieutenant Granta's idea."

"Granta!" Hemenez nodded as he lit his cheroot and blew the smoke in Brogan's direction. "*Si*, I should have guessed, Colonel Sanchez does not have the brains. So, you have been sent here. Why have you been sent here?"

"To lure you into a trap," said Brogan, deciding that the direct approach was the best.

"A trap!" laughed Hemenez. It is a fine trap you set if you tell me that is what you intend to do."

"I suspect that Granta knew I would tell you," said Brogan. "Maybe he thinks that the bait is irresistible."

"And what could possibly make it so?"

"Money, gold," said Brogan.

"Money and gold is always a very tempting bait," admitted Hemenez. "How does Granta intend to use it as bait to trap me?"

"I'm to tell you that there is a big shipment leavin' Santa Cruz in three days and that it is going to the military garrison at Cuidad Juarez — wherever that is — along the valley of the Rio Negro."

"How big?" asked Hemenez.

"That I don't know," said Brogan. "All I know is it's supposed to be a big shipment."

Hemenez smiled and nodded. "The lieutenant did not lie to you," he said. "I have spies in many places and they have already informed me that such a shipment is due to take place. The only thing they did not know was when. Such information is kept very secret and the first the ordinary soldier knows of it is when they are assembled and marched off."

"You have spies in the army?" asked Brogan.

Hemenez grinned broadly "Not all the soldiers are willing volunteers. There are many who have been forced into service, many who come from towns such as Santa Cruz."

"Does that include any of Granta's men?"

Hemenez grinned again but shook his head. "No, they are special. They are all carefully selected volunteers. These are truly soldiers to be feared."

"I thought so," said Brogan. "Anyhow, that's it. I was sent to tell you about the shipment and somehow persuade you to attack it."

"But you are free, *gringo*," said Hemenez. "There was nothing to stop you leaving Mexico and going home — wherever home is to you. Why did you not just ride on, choose a different route?"

Brogan nodded and admitted that if he had any sense at all that's just what he ought to have done and then told the *bandido* what had happened in Santa Cruz, including the executions.

When Brogan had finished talking, Hemenez cursed in Spanish; it was obviously cursing even though Brogan did not speak the language, some things translate very easily.

"There was a rumour that such a thing had happened," sighed Hemenez eventually. "I fear that my father and sister were among the dead. That is why this village was chosen, because of me. Many of them are related to me."

"Well they're all dead now," said Brogan.

"And for that alone both Sanchez and Granta must die. The gold is no longer important."

"Granta didn't have nothin' to do with the slaughter," Brogan pointed out.

"It was his men who carried out the executions, you told me so," said Hemenez.

"He was just obeyin' orders," said Brogan, wondering why he was suddenly defending the lieutenant.

"Granta is more dangerous than Colonel Sanchez," Hemenez grated, spitting on to the floor. "Very well, *gringo*, you have done what you set out to do. The question now is what do I do about you? The men you injured in Santa Cruz are of one mind, you must die."

"But you're not so sure?" suggested Brogan.

Hemenez shrugged and spat on to the floor again. "What happens to you

134

is no concern of mine," he said. "*Si*, it is true, I do not like Americano *gringos*, but you have proved yourself different from most. Even so, whether you die or not does not matter to me at all. I should just hand you over to my men and let them do as they will with you and I can assure you that it would be a most painful end."

"And are you goin' to?"

Hemenez suddenly laughed. "As things are at this moment I would die before you. I have seen that you sit in such a position that you could get your gun long before I could reach for mine. No, *gringo*, I am not so stupid as to believe that I could outdraw or outgun you and I value my own life too much to even think about risking such a thing. No, as far as I am concerned you are free to go but I cannot answer for any of my men and I shall make no attempt to stop them."

"I guess I know where I stand," said Brogan. "Only thing is I don't think I could just leave right now on account of Anna an' Padre Miguel."

Hemenez laughed and shook his head. "Honour is one luxury I gave up a long time ago, *gringo*. So they die, what is it to you? They die, you are free and being free is what matters to you, the reason you choose the life you do."

"Don't know 'bout no honour," said Brogan. "All I know is I made me a promise to help them if I could an' I ain't about to run out now."

"It is your choice, *gringo*." said Hemenez. "I find it refreshing that someone like you should wish to help. Very well, I make you this promise. As long as you are my guest I will not allow anyone to kill you. Other than that I cannot control what happens."

"Can't say fairer'n that," nodded Brogan. "So what are you goin' to do about the money an' gold?"

Once again Hemenez laughed. "*Gringo*, since you come here to invite me into a trap, I feel that I cannot refuse such an invitation. We shall attack them and take the gold."

136

"I hope you know what you're doin'!"

Apart from the two men Brogan had injured in Santa Cruz, everyone else in the camp was quite friendly, some even asking about relatives they had in America and seemed quite disappointed when he had to admit that he did not know them. Most did not seem to be able to grasp the fact that the American way of life was completely different to theirs and could not really grasp the concept of the army not being involved in everyday life.

Food, although plain and simple, seemed plentiful and morale high. However, despite the air of well-being, it was painfully obvious to Brogan that when it came to the purely practical act of being welded into a fighting force capable of taking on the army, enthusiasm far outweighed ability.

Pablo Hemenez and his men were

doing their best to train the men in the use of guns and whilst there were one or two who showed ability, the majority seemed either over-awed by their weapons or tended to treat the occasion like some sort of good-humoured game.

"You can't seriously think about attackin' them soldiers?" queried Brogan. "You'd be wiped off the face of the earth."

Hemenez laughed and nodded in agreement. "*Si*, you are right. In an open battle they would stand no chance, but it is not my plan to face the soldiers head on."

"Ambush?"

"*Si*, ambush," nodded Hemenez.

Brogan looked at some men being instructed in the use of rifles as they attempted to hit stones placed on rocks and did not see one shot hit its target.

"I'd say the soldiers were pretty safe," he observed. "Maybe with more time one or two of 'em might hit somethin' occasionally."

"Time!" sighed Hemenez. "*Si*, time! However, in this case time is something we do not have but we are badly in need of money to buy more guns and it is not often that an opportunity such as this presents itself. A rabble they may be, but all are agreed that they must try. For them it is a matter of honour."

"And for you?" asked Brogan.

Hemenez laughed. "For me it is a way of life." He looked hard at Brogan for a few moments. "*Gringo*," he said eventually, "it is plain that you think we do not have any chance . . . " He sighed heavily. "*Si*, I must agree with you. A small body of soldiers perhaps we can deal with since most of them are in sympathy with us already, but Lieutenant Granta and his men are not as ordinary soldiers, they are highly trained killers. However, we need that money if we are to have any hope of ever throwing off the shackles of oppression. I know that the lieutenant offers the gold as bait and he also knows that we are bound to try and steal it."

"Maybe so," agreed Brogan, "but the whole object is to either kill or capture you and even you must admit that you'd be puttin' your head into a noose."

"So have you any other ideas, *gringo*?" sighed Hemenez.

"I've been thinkin' about that since yesterday," said Brogan. "Don't see why the hell I should bother though."

"Because you have a strange sense of honour, my friend," smiled Hemenez. "You have made a promise to Anna and Padre Miguel and no matter what happens you must try to honour that promise."

"I could still just ride out."

Hemenez grinned and slapped Brogan on the back. "Had such a thing been your intention you would have continued your journey yesterday. Come, *gringo*, share your thoughts with a simple Mexican *bandido*."

"Well, I got me to thinkin' that

Granta ain't about to risk losin' that money no matter what his intentions were. Even he knows there's a chance that somethin' might not go quite right an' he'd end up losin' it an' that'd be one sure way of him endin' up in front of a firin' squad himself. I reckon that the money — if there is any — will be sent on by a different route."

"I am quite certain that the money is there," assured Hemenez. "As I say, I have spies in the army and they have confirmed this some time ago."

"OK, so the money is there," conceded Brogan. "You know the country, what other way could they go from Santa Cruz?"

Hemenez thought for a moment. "There is another way," he said eventually, "but it would mean at least another day on the journey. From Santa Cruz they could go through the pass and then turn west over the Sierra Madres. It is not easy but it can be done. The trail eventually leads on to the trail from the Rio Negro but well past any possible ambush points."

"Then why don't they use it more often?" asked Brogan.

"Because it is so difficult," said Hemenez. "For much of the journey through the sierras it is barely wide enough for the wagons. There is a very steep drop on one side and an impossible climb on the other. It would need only one slip of the foot or for one wheel to go over the edge to fall to certain death and the track is very rough."

"Then that's the way he's goin' to send it!" declared Brogan. "Sure, he'll make a show about it bein' with him. How far is it to the trail from here?"

"By leaving now we could be in position by the morning," said Hemenez. "But it would mean riding for most of the night."

"Not 'we'," corrected Brogan, "I told you once before that I ain't never stolen nothin' off nobody an' I don't intend to start now, not even from the Mexican Army. All I'm sayin' is that if you

142

want that gold you've got to take it. I'll guarantee that's the way he'll be sendin' it."

"You are indeed a strange man," sighed Hemenez. "And just what will you be doing?"

"I'll give you time to get into position, wait for Granta to go through the Rio Negro an' then head back to Santa Cruz."

"And do what?"

"I won't know about that until I get there," admitted Brogan. "I guess I'll just have to wait an' see what develops."

Hemenez thought long and hard but seemed unable to reach a decision on what to do. He even called in an elderly peon and for about ten minutes they carried on an animated conversation in Spanish.

"He is of the same mind as me," sighed Hemenez when the conversation ended and the man left. "For us to attempt to take the money either in the valley of the Rio Negro or along the trail through the Sierra Madres would be suicide. Lieutenant Granta is devious enough to send what appears to be the gold through the sierras when it is really being sent through the Rio Negro. On the other hand he could send it that way and hope we believe it is going along the Rio Negro."

"Looks like you've got yourself one hell of a problem," grinned Brogan. "My money would be on takin' it through the mountains."

"I am inclined to agree with you," nodded Hemenez. "But we cannot be certain."

"It makes sense to me," said Brogan. "Granta is a very ambitious man and even he wouldn't dare riskin' the shipment bein' lost or stolen, he knows he'd end up in front of a firin' squad if he did lose it. So he makes a show of it comin' through this Rio Negro when it's really goin' the other way."

"Even if you are right, *gringo*," grunted Hemenez, "it does not help us. I have only six men who are able to fight, who have the instinct for it. The others are very willing but they are all inexperienced and I know in my heart that most would turn and run as soon as things became difficult. They are not mountain men, they are farmers. Besides, we do not have that many good guns, perhaps thirty at the most."

"Then it looks like you've got to forget all about the money," said Brogan. "Granta will be disappointed but at least you'll still be alive to do what you can another day and Granta will get his gold through."

"It is this thought which upsets me," said Hemenez. "I would dearly like to see the lieutenant disgraced. There would be only one thing better and that would be to kill him myself. Besides, *gringo*, he has issued a challenge and no *bandido* worth anything would refuse such a challenge."

"Thought you said honour was a luxury you gave up a long time ago," reminded Brogan.

"Honour!" exclaimed Hemenez. "What has this to do with honour? It is a matter of pride, of my standing. Granta will have made it plain that he has issued me with a challenge and should I refuse he will quickly spread the word that I was too frightened."

"Honour, pride, what's the difference?" said Brogan. "Like I said, at least you'll still be alive."

Hemenez sank into a deep, almost self-pitying thoughtful sulk for a few minutes but suddenly he smiled. "Mérida!" he exclaimed jumping to his feet. "*Si*, I have the answer; Mérida, we must go at once to Mérida."

Brogan had wondered just who or what Mérida was and now he realized that it must be a place. "I take it this Mérida is somewhere you think you can ambush the money," he said.

"Of course!" declared Hemenez. "Fool that I am not to have thought about it before. Mérida is a village on the road to Cuidad Juarez, one that

146

is used regularly by the army as an overnight stop. The villagers are all against the army."

"How does that help you?" asked Brogan. "No disrespect to any Mexican, but it seems to me almost all of 'em take the easy way out whether they like it or not."

Hemenez laughed. "You understand the peon well, *gringo*. I have many peons here but it is impossible to turn all but a few of them into fighting men."

"And you hope to use men like this against a highly organized force like Lieutenant Granta's?"

"They will not be necessary," said Hemenez. "I shall take the best of them and my own men — and you . . . "

"I'd take it kindly if'n you'd just leave me out of it," said Brogan. "I said before I ain't never stolen nothin' off nobody an' I don't intend to make the Mexican Army an exception."

"The choice is yours, *gringo*," smiled Hemenez. "You come with me or I have you killed here. It really does not matter to me if you die or not, but I have a certain admiration for you and am prepared to give you a chance."

"What you want me along for anyhow?"

"Because even though I have a certain amount of admiration for you, I do not trust you, *gringo*. I would be much happier if you were where I could see you. How am I to know that if I leave you here you will not ride somewhere to meet Lieutenant Granta and inform him what I am doing? Indeed it could be that you have arranged such a meeting."

"Don't suppose my word that I haven't any such meeting arranged would be good enough?"

"You are quite right, *gringo*, your word would not be good enough. Sleep well tonight, we leave in the morning at dawn."

"I always sleep well," said Brogan. "That's 'cos I've got a clear conscience."

Hemenez suddenly turned, his gun

148

pointing at Brogan. "I too have a clear conscience, *gringo*. It would not trouble my conscience at all to shoot you. Your guns, *gringo*, I do not trust you not to escape during the night. You will be tied up and guarded. Your guns will be returned to you in the morning."

Brogan sighed and knew that Pablo Hemenez would be as good as his word and have no qualms about killing him if he chose not to obey and he was not ready to die just yet. He grudgingly handed over his long barrelled Colt which Hemenez looked at admiringly, testing its weight and feel.

"A fine weapon!" he said. "Perhaps too good for a hobo."

"Just make sure I get it back in the mornin'," growled Brogan.

"Or else what?" jibed Hemenez. "I would suggest that you are hardly in a position to bargain or make threats. Do not worry, it shall be returned to you."

From that moment on a guard was posted outside the hut and followed

Brogan about wherever he went. At about nine o'clock one of Hemenez's regular men came into the hut and made a good job of tying Brogan up.

7

TRUE to his word, Pablo Hemenez handed back the Colt as they mounted up. Brogan checked his saddle-bags and was somewhat surprised to find that the contents, such as they were, appeared to be intact.

"How long will it take to reach this Mérida?" he asked.

"We shall be in position by midnight at the latest," said Hemenez. "We must ride hard and long, stopping only to rest and water the horses. The way is hard across the mountains and there is no road to follow. It will not be easy; are you sure that that old horse of yours will not die underneath you?"

"Sure as I can be," said Brogan. "You just lead the way, me an' her'll follow."

Brogan counted thirty-two men, not

including himself, most still in the garb of the peons they were, but at least they looked a little more self-assured and at home with rifles than the majority. At first they chattered excitedly as they set off, but after a very short time their enthusiasm had subsided and only the occasional word or laugh could be heard.

Pablo Hemenez had not understated himself when he had said it would be hard going. At first thick clumps of coarse grass made it difficult for the horses to find a firm footing, although this gave way after about an hour to shorter grass but rather more boggy underneath. After another two hours they started to climb on to firmer, more open ground and their pace increased rapidly.

In the mountains, although firm underfoot, they had to negotiate frequent fast-flowing streams, deep ravines and many wet and slippery slopes all of which threatened to deprive them of more than one horse and rider, though all survived somehow.

In all they made four stops, each of no more than fifteen minutes duration but Brogan began to have serious doubts as to whether they would reach the village of Mérida since he could not see them clearing the mountains before nightfall. Hemenez though kept on looking up at the sky, maintaining that they would be clear by dusk. In the event they did clear the mountains just as it turned dark.

"We have made good time," declared Hemenez as they descended on to a flat, dry, treeless plain. "We should reach Mérida in about three hours."

They had stopped beside a small water-hole, the water warm, brown and of doubtful flavour after the clear water of the mountains but most drank it. A few, Brogan included, decided that they could survive until they reached Mérida.

"So what's your plan?" Brogan asked.

"It is simple, *gringo*," laughed

153

Hemenez. "We take over the town, have men stationed in each of the houses and when the money arrives, we shoot the soldiers from the cover of the houses."

"That simple!" smiled Brogan.

"*Si*, it is as simple as that," replied Hemenez. "The town, she is set around a square. The soldiers ride in from the east and immediately they have no cover, they are shot at from all sides. There will be no survivors."

"Hope you don't mind if I say it sounds too easy," said Brogan.

Hemenez laughed. "*Gringo*, I would remind you that this is not America. The mind of the Mexican is different to that of the Americano. I understand what you are trying to say, that such things have a habit of turning out not to be so simple. In your country, perhaps so. It will be easy, you will see."

Brogan had to admit that life did not seem so complicated in Mexico and that the average peon seemed incapable of taking in anything too complex, but he also knew from experience that this was not necessarily correct. Even so, he could not help his feeling that everything was not as straightforward as Hemenez seemed to think.

* * *

Hemenez was almost exact with his timing as they arrived above the village of Mérida a little over three hours later. The moon was high and full, giving them a clear view over the village from a clifftop some forty feet above.

A few lights could be seen in one or two windows and a dog sensed their presence and started to bark, causing several other dogs to join in. The scene was much as Hemenez had described it, houses surrounding a square on four sides, but one thing struck Brogan as unusual, although he had come across it before — there was no church.

Hemenez pulled his men back from the edge of the cliff and led them about half a mile further along where there was a way down, a fairly steep cutting through the face of the cliff. As they had withdrawn Brogan had heard various voices urging their dogs to be quiet but there was something about the voices that made Brogan's senses cry out.

"Somethin's wrong," he said to Hemenez before they descended on to the trail below.

"Wrong, *gringo*?" laughed Hemenez. "What is there to be wrong?"

"The way them folk told their dogs to shut up, almost as if they were frightened of something an' don't tell me it was just because their dogs started to bark. I don't like it, somethin' tells me there's somethin' else an' it ain't often my senses are wrong."

Hemenez laughed again. "What is there that could possibly be wrong? You have seen for yourself that the village is quiet, just as it should be at this time of night. You worry too much. You will see, we shall take over the houses and wait for the soldiers and all will be well."

"I wish I had your confidence," grunted Brogan.

"*Gringo*," snapped Hemenez, "if you are frightened, remain here until we have done what we have to." He motioned his men down the cutting and laughed again. Brogan decided to pay heed to his own feelings and did not follow them.

He rode back along the cliff and looked down on the village as Hemenez and his band rode slowly in and dismounted. He saw Hemenez gather them together and point in various directions and the men scattered to enter the houses. He was forced to admit that perhaps this time his senses had betrayed him as everything appeared to go according to plan. When all the men had entered the houses, he idly urged his horse forward along the cliff to the far end of the village and suddenly he knew that his senses had not betrayed him.

* * *

Below him, in a rough corral at the base of the cliff and fairly well hidden, the sudden snort of horses attracted his attention and, dismounting and creeping forward to peer over the cliff, he saw at least forty horses, possibly fifty — it was difficult to count them in the half light.

"Unless they is very well-off peons," he muttered to himself, "they could never afford horses like that."

There was another movement immediately below him and this time he could make out the dim shape of two human figures and there was absolutely no doubt that these men were soldiers. The men moved amongst the horses and quietened them down, but did not look up.

"Looks like they walked straight into a trap," Brogan said to himself. "Question is, what do I do now?"

His problem appeared to be solved for him as he heard a voice calling and it was plainly not calling to the two soldiers in the corral. At the same time another soldier suddenly appeared from the direction of the village, this time running, and spoke to the two in the corral. There was a brief cheer followed by laughter. The voice called out again and somehow Brogan knew it was directed at him. He led his horse back along the cliff until he was above the village again and looked down, making no attempt to hide himself.

A vaguely familiar figure stood in the square looking up at him and called again.

"Señor McNally!" called the familiar voice of Lieutenant Granta. "You can come down, you have done well, they are all under arrest."

"I reckon I'm safer up here," Brogan called.

"No need!" assured Granta. "I can assure you that you are now free to go where you choose. I am a man of my word, Mr McNally, but it would be foolish of you to refuse my hospitality at this time of night. Please, trust me, you will come to no harm, I have news for you."

"What the hell!" muttered Brogan. "I guess I can't lose anythin'." He called out again. "I hear what you say, Lieutenant. OK, this time I'm goin' to trust you, I'm comin' down."

"A wise decision," replied Granta. "I shall be in the first house over there . . ." He pointed to a corner of the square. "There is food and drink for you."

Brogan mounted his horse and urged her forward to the cutting and down into the village. As he arrived he was in time to see men being pushed out into the square, this time with their hands tied firmly behind their backs and all looking very dejected. Pablo Hemenez did not appear to be among them.

Other soldiers were now collecting the *bandidos'* horses and leading them towards the corral. The *bandidos* too were being pushed to the far end of the village, Brogan presumed to some place where they could be kept securely. Nobody made any attempt to take Brogan or his horse and he tied her to a post outside the house indicated by Lieutenant Granta, looked about for a few moments and then marched in without knocking.

He was met by the terrified faces of, he assumed, the owner of the house and his wife huddled in a corner and Lieutenant Granta sitting at a rough table in the process of pouring a colourless liquid into a glass.

Granta smiled, indicated a chair and pushed the bottle towards Brogan.

"Have a drink, Mr McNally," he said. "It is rough but more than welcome on a cold night such as this."

"No thanks," replied Brogan, sitting down. "I like to keep a clear head."

"You do not seem surprised to see me," grinned the lieutenant.

"I got over bein' surprised at anythin' a long time ago," grunted Brogan. "I had the feelin' you was here."

161

"So Hemenez tells me," laughed Granta. "I am glad that he did not listen to you, it could have made life difficult."

Brogan looked about, saw two small faces peering through a curtain that covered a hole in one wall which served as a bed and another small child appeared briefly from behind its mother.

"Where is he, Hemenez?" he asked. "I didn't see him outside with the others."

"Señor Hemenez is enjoying my hospitality in a cellar," grinned the Lieutenant. "Why do you ask, are you concerned for his welfare?"

"About as concerned as I would be for a cockroach," said Brogan. "Just curious, that's all."

The two men looked at each other for a few moments, Brogan looking impassive and Granta smiling slightly. Eventually Granta sighed and spoke.

"You are a most difficult man to understand. It seems to me that you

162

are not at all interested in knowing how we came to be here."

"I figure you'll tell me when it suits you," replied Brogan. "Didn't you say somethin' about some food?"

The lieutenant laughed. "Is that all you have to say? *Si*, there is food and very good it is too, very Mexican but very good." He spoke to the woman in Spanish and she grudgingly got to her feet and went through into a small room at the rear. "Very well, Mr McNally, since you do not ask, I will tell you how we came to be here. Even if you do not care, it will give me pleasure to tell you and show that all Mexicans are not fools."

"Is that the news you had for me?" Brogan yawned deliberately. "You said you had news for me."

"News!" smiled Granta. "Ah, yes, that. Very well, I shall start with the news. Do you remember Colonel Sanchez and the minister . . . ?"

"All too clearly," grunted Brogan. "I remember a whole lot of peons bein'

163

slaughtered for nothin' as well."

"Executed!" corrected the lieutenant. "However we could argue about the rights and wrongs of that affair for the rest of our lives. Since you must know that it was on the colonel's orders that they were executed, it will no doubt give you great satisfaction to hear that Colonel Sanchez is no more."

"No more?" queried Brogan.

"Dead!" smiled Granta. "Both he and the minister were killed the day they left Santa Cruz. Oh, nothing to do with the *bandidos* or the rebels. The coach they were riding in went out of control and they crashed down a deep ravine; they both died instantly."

"You don't seem too upset at the news," nodded Brogan. "Me, I guess I'm glad in a way, but it really don't matter that much."

The lieutenant laughed. "I too must confess that I have lost no sleep over it. Colonel Sanchez did not like me and I did not like him. There is another thing as far I am concerned, and that is I am due for promotion and I know Sanchez would have done anything to see that I did not get it."

"Congratulations," muttered Brogan. "You didn't have anythin' to do with his death, did you?"

"A most unworthy observation," grinned the lieutenant. "It would be as well if others did not think the same. However, there you have my news and here comes your food."

The woman appeared with two bowls, one full of rice and the other full of a spicy looking stew. Neither appealed to Brogan very much but he knew that it was all he was going to get.

"Water?" he asked of the woman, raising his hand to his mouth in a drinking motion.

"*Si*, water," responded the woman returning to the back room and reemerging with a jar and a mug. She set the mug down and poured out some water. "Some bread?" she asked.

"You speak English," smiled Brogan. "Sure, if you have any."

"I speak a little Americano," she said, smiling weakly. She produced some rather stale bread and returned to her husband and child.

"I can see that you do not care for Mexican food all that much," smiled Granta. "I must confess that it took me some time to adapt to it after eating English food. Now, I will tell you how I came to be here."

"I'm listenin'," grunted Brogan as he dipped a piece of bread into the stew and sucked the juice. "Seems I ain't got much choice in the matter."

"I am hurt that you do not seem interested," complained the lieutenant. "However, I shall continue. It is no accident that we chose this village, I had made the decision before you left. I did not really believe that Hemenez would dare to attack a large body of troops no matter how many peons he had under his command. I also knew that he was aware of the route through

166

the Sierra Madres and that the gold might go that way."

"An' which way did you send it?" slurped Brogan through a mouthful of rice and stew.

The lieutenant laughed. "It did not go either way. Two hours after you had left Santa Cruz, a messenger arrived to say that the shipment had been cancelled. However, since neither you nor Hemenez were in a position to know, I decided to go ahead with my plan. I knew also that you would tell Hemenez that I was setting a trap in the knowledge that this too would make him go to Mérida."

Somehow Brogan found that he was not at all surprised and nodded knowingly. "How long have you been here?" he asked.

"We rode out of Santa Cruz about an hour after the messenger arrived. There is a third way which avoids both the Rio Negro and the Sierra Madres, but it is over the mountains. We came that way."

Brogan spooned a heap of stew into his mouth and nodded as he ate. "It figures," he slurped again. "I said you was a devious an' dangerous cuss."

"From you, I shall take that as a compliment," smiled Granta. "You are indeed a very hard man to impress."

"Anyone tryin' to impress me is wastin' their time," Brogan grinned. "Even if I am, an' it happens sometimes, I try my best not to show it."

"Perhaps you have a point," agreed the lieutenant. "I do not share your inhibitions; if someone impresses me I say so and I must admit that I am impressed by you. Not the way you look, smell or live, I find you most strange in that way. I am impressed by your ability to sense danger, to know what is ahead."

"I guess that's "cos of the way I look, smell an' live!" Brogan grinned.

"*Touché!*" nodded Granta. "That's French and means you have scored the point. It is a fencing term I believe."

"Only fencin' I know about is the

ones they have round farms an' ranches," said Brogan.

"I would imagine so," grinned the lieutenant. "Hemenez says he should have listened to you when you told him that all was not right. Tell me, Mr McNally, how *did* you know that something was wrong, did you see the horses?"

Brogan looked thoughtful. "Guess I must've heard 'em," he said. "Can't actually remember hearin' 'em then. No, at the time it was more to do with the way them dogs barked an' the way they was shut up. Folk is usually louder an' harder when they tell dogs to keep quiet, either that or they let 'em bark an' come out to find out what the hell they is barkin' about. Yeh, that was it, nobody came out. Folk almost allus come out to see what's happenin', usually with a gun."

"And that was all?" asked Granta, slightly disbelieving.

"No," admitted Brogan. "When you've been travellin' as long as I have, your life can often depend on nothin' else than a gut feelin'. It becomes a sort of sense an' in my case it ain't often wrong. I had me this feelin' as soon as we got here."

The lieutenant sighed and shook his head. "I could use a man like you as a scout," he said. "I am sure it could be arranged."

"No thanks," said Brogan. "I'm a loner an' intend stayin' that way."

"In a way I envy you," said Granta. "No orders to obey, no responsibilities and you can come and go as you please."

"An' be arrested by the Mexican Army, an' have almost every lawman look at you as though you just crept out from under a stone, an' have folk spit on the ground when they see you, an' have everyone assume that you steal everythin', an' if somethin' goes wrong when you're around it's bound to be down to you." Brogan smiled. "You want more?"

"It is one of the disadvantages of the

life. You choose," smiled the lieutenant. He called out in Spanish and a soldier bustled in and stood to attention as Granta gave him an order. "I have sent for Hemenez," he explained. "I wish for him to see that you are free."

"Can't see as that'll do any good," said Brogan spooning the last of the stew and rice into his mouth.

"It will give me satisfaction," smiled Granta, "and it is always good for me to be satisfied."

Brogan nodded and slowly chewed on the food in his mouth. A few minutes later, the door opened and a dirty, bleeding figure was pushed into the room where he blinked in the unaccustomed light. He had obviously taken quite a beating, the blood now congealed around several cuts on his face. He blinked again and suddenly grinned.

"*Gringo*!" he rasped, hoarsely. "It is good to see you again." He looked at the bowls and at the jug of water and licked his lips. "I see that they treat you well. They do not treat me or my men well, some water would be most welcome."

Brogan nodded and without asking for permission, topped up the mug and handed it to the *bandido*. The lieutenant smiled indulgently and did not interfere.

"Told you there was somethin' wrong," said Brogan.

"Indeed you did, *gringo*," grinned Hemenez as water dribbled down his chin. "I was very foolish, I should have listened to you. They were waiting for us as we entered the houses, we did not stand a chance."

"You'll know better next time," said Brogan.

"There will be no next time," assured the lieutenant. "The execution of Pablo Hemenez and all the other *bandidos* will take place in public with everyone we can muster being forced to watch. It will serve as a warning to others."

"Don't he even get a trial?" asked Brogan.

The lieutenant laughed loudly. "A trial! What purpose will such a thing serve? They are all *bandidos*; everyone knows that so what would a trial prove?"

"Where I come from everybody has the right to a trial," said Brogan, "no matter what they've done."

"I know," agreed Granta. "I am an admirer of your system, but it does not apply in Mexico. It is a fact which neither you nor I can do anything about."

"Guess not," Brogan shrugged. "I hope you don't mind if I don't watch the execution."

"The choice is yours," smiled the lieutenant.

"When?" Brogan asked again.

"When we return to Santa Cruz," said the lieutenant. "Padre Miguel and your precious Anna will be forced to witness the event."

"Then I'd better get back there an' take my leave of them before that happens."

"Are you afraid to witness an execution?" grinned Hemenez.

"No," said Brogan, "I seen enough to last me a lifetime, that's all."

Suddenly there was a lot of noise outside and shortly afterwards a soldier burst breathlessly into the room, saluted briefly and spoke to the lieutenant in Spanish.

Pablo Hemenez threw his head back and roared with laughter and Lieutenant Granta's expression changed to one of pure rage. He jumped to his feet and bounded to the door where he barked an order at someone. The soldier bearing the message looked a little bewildered and eventually decided that a retreat was in order under the cover of the ensuing mayhem.

"I didn't understand a word of what they said," said Brogan to Hemenez, "but my guess is that someone has escaped."

Once again Hemenez laughed. "*Si, gringo*, four of my best men. They overpowered a guard, killed him and took some horses. The lieutenant is wasting his time trying to organize anyone to go after them. They know this country far better than he or his men."

"I ain't too sure if that's a good or bad thing," said Brogan. "From your point of view it could be that Granta will execute you right here."

"It is possible," nodded Hemenez, "but I do not believe so. I am too valuable a prize; he needs to make an example of me to the peons."

"Do you think they'll try to free you?"

"They must!" asserted Hemenez.

"What the hell for?" Brogan asked. "They're free, you're not!"

8

LIEUTENANT GRANTA returned, plainly in a rage, saw Hemenez and Brogan and appeared to become even more enraged as he turned and roared some instructions. A few seconds later two soldiers hurried in and dragged the *bandido* to his feet. One of the soldiers looked at Brogan and then questioningly at his superior who indicated that Brogan was to be left alone. Hemenez was dragged outside, still laughing and even though it was obvious that he was being beaten, continued to laugh. Eventually he was dragged away and bundled into a cellar which was then securely locked and placed under the guard of four soldiers. Brogan smiled and did not envy the men their task. If Pablo Hemenez should escape it would be their lives which would be forfeit.

He had been watching the scene from a window but when the lieutenant returned he was sitting at the table pouring himself a glass of the clear liquid which Granta had first offered him. He raised the glass in salute.

"Just goes to show that even the best of plans can go wrong," he said, taking a sip of the liquid and grimacing as it burned its way down his throat. He smacked his lips. "Rough!" he exclaimed. "What they use it for, killin' rats?"

The lieutenant ignored the remark and crashed down into a chair, all the time cursing in Spanish. Brogan decided to allow Granta to come to his senses in his own time, drank the remainder of the rat poison in his glass and for some reason decided to refill it. After about five minutes Granta's rage seemed to subside and he snatched the glass off Brogan and poured himself a measure of the rat poison.

"I sometimes think that I am in

command of a bunch of fools!" he growled. "I gave instructions for four men to guard the prisoners but it appears that there were only two. Now one of them is dead and the other badly injured."

"You can't blame them," said Brogan, "at least they was there."

"I do not blame them," sighed Granta. "However, Sergeant Ortaga has some questions to answer." He drained the glass, coughed and spluttered a little and poured out another measure which he looked at dubiously. "Perhaps you are right, Mr McNally, perhaps this is more useful as rat poison." However, he drained the glass in one gulp and wheezed as it burned into his chest and stomach. "Unfortunately I must postpone my questioning of the sergeant. It is now more important than ever that I get the others, especially Hemenez, back to Santa Cruz. We leave at dawn. Since it is also your desire to see Anna and Padre Miguel, it would seem churlish of you not to accompany us."

"If'n I knew what 'churlish' meant, I might agree with you," said Brogan. "If it means that I might as well ride with you, I'll agree with that."

"Then have a good sleep, Mr McNally," said Granta, smiling for the first time. I suggest that you find yourself a woman for the night."

Brogan made it clear that he was not looking for any company during the night and went out to find his horse still tethered to the hitching post where he had left her.

He had seen what appeared to be a barn alongside the corral and led his horse there and, much to his surprise, found the building occupied by only two goats. The goats smelled but that did not put Brogan off and they in turn did not appear to object to the smell of Brogan.

★ ★ ★

The prisoners were put on their horses and their hands tied to the horns of their saddles in front of them. All except Pablo Hemenez were surrounded by heavily armed soldiers but Hemenez was made to ride just behind Brogan and the lieutenant.

"It is just to ensure that if anything happens, he will be among the first to die," explained Granta. "He knows this and the men who escaped know it too, so they will not risk anything."

"I guess you know what you're doin'," said Brogan. "Lead on, I'll just follow."

"You may never reach Santa Cruz," laughed Hemenez.

"You had better hope that we do," said Granta, turning and smiling at his prisoner. "At the first sign of anyone attempting to attack us, I shall see to it that my first bullet finds its way into your head."

"If you intend to shoot me when we get there," laughed Hemenez, "I do not see that it matters. Being dead in the mountains is no different to me to being dead in Santa Cruz."

"I agree with him," said Brogan. "Dead is dead no matter how or where it happens."

The lieutenant laughed. "The difference is that while he is still alive he always has hope."

"And you enjoy seein' a man clingin' to hope?" asked Brogan.

"I enjoy seeing men like Hemenez suffer," said Granta. "Anyway, I do not think that four men would dare to take on forty, they are not exactly favourable odds."

"An' I suppose you do have a lot of hostages," said Brogan.

The lieutenant laughed. "Were it just the peons behind us, I do not think they would give a damn, the only man they would be concerned about is their leader, Pablo Hemenez. They need him, they do not have the brains to think for themselves."

Brogan was inclined to agree with

Lieutenant Granta's assessment of the *bandidos*.

* * *

After about an hour they left the main trail and headed off towards the mountains. At first the going was quite easy, although it would have been impossible for a wagon to negotiate the terrain, which explained why the trail had never been built that way.

They had to negotiate several very steep and narrow paths down the sides of deep ravines but despite this, Granta seemed to think that they were making good progress.

Santa Cruz was reached without incident and most of the townsfolk turned out to see just who was among the prisoners. Some appeared to be relatives although Brogan did discover that none were the husbands or sons of anyone in town.

The arrival of the soldiers was greeted with almost total silence and it even took Padre Miguel and Anna a lot of effort to acknowledge Brogan. Brogan sought them out a few minutes later.

"Yet more slaughter!" sighed Padre Miguel. "Can there be no end to it?"

"Maybe that's a question you must ask your God," said Brogan. "Seems to me if He's as all-powerful as you reckon, then He ought to do somethin'."

"Faith!" replied the padre, rather sadly.

"Which is why I prefer this!" Brogan smiled and patted the Colt at his hip.

"God works his wonders in mysterious ways," nodded the padre. "Perhaps He even uses such as you."

"He ain't never told me about it if He has," smiled Brogan. "Anyhow, the point is both you an' Anna should be safe now. I reckon I can leave first thing in the mornin'."

"You had your chance to leave us," smiled Anna. "I still say that your horse knew better than you, but I am glad that you chose not to just forget us."

"Sorry about the others," said Brogan. "There's absolutely nothin' I can do about them, even if I wanted to."

"You have already done far more than any other man would have done," smiled Anna. "Do not blame yourself for what you cannot do."

★ ★ ★

They had been standing in the doorway of the church and for more than two hours the prisoners had been kept standing in the square in the heat of the sun. Two of them had collapsed of heat exhaustion and the padre, Anna and a couple of other women were ushered away when they attempted to help. Now, an hour later, the two bodies were being carried away by the soldiers who declared the men to be dead. This time Padre Miguel was allowed to attend them and he too confirmed their death.

After another hour, during which time Brogan was forced to retreat to the padre house for coolness, two more men collapsed and were eventually carried away, again both dead. Lieutenant Granta came into the house and smiled.

"I have sent men out to the outlying villages to bring everyone to witness the executions," he told the padre. "Examples have to be made if we are to maintain law and order."

"Seems to me if you keep them poor folk standin' out there in this heat much longer you won't have anyone left to make an example of," said Brogan.

"Your concern is noted," sneered Granta. "As a matter of fact, if you look out you will see that they are even now being taken away somewhere sheltered where they will be given water. There is little point in wasting good food on them since they are to die."

"When?" asked Brogan.

"Tomorrow morning," said Granta. "I have decided that you will not be allowed to leave until after the executions. Do not worry, after that you will be free to go."

"Thanks for nothin'!" growled Brogan.

"Things could have turned out much worse for you," said the lieutenant. "You could so easily have been killed that first day we captured you, in fact you almost were and certainly would have been had Colonel Sanchez had his way."

"Worse!" exclaimed Brogan. "Thirty innocent people dead already an' about another thirty lined up to be killed. I'd say things was bad enough."

"But it is you who are still alive," grinned the lieutenant. "That fact alone must be most satisfactory to you." Brogan shrugged and consoled himself with the thought that it would have happened had he been there or not. "Already they arrive from other villages," Granta continued. "It is a pity that I did not think to bring along the people from Mérida, but it is too far away to do anything about that oversight now."

Brogan and Anna looked out of the window to see a group of about fifteen peons being herded into the square where, after a brief talk by a soldier, they broke up and wandered off to various houses where they were ushered in and the doors firmly closed.

From then on, peons seemed to be arriving at regular intervals, again all being taken in by the citizens of Santa Cruz. Even Anna opened up her house to as many as she could accommodate and, when it was plain that there was simply no more room to be had in any house or barn, Padre Miguel, somewhat reluctantly, opened up the church. The last of the peons arrived at about ten in the evening and were accommodated here. Brogan did note that although the padre had opened up the church, he had not taken anyone into his house but it was not until he raised the point that he realized that the people had refused to put the priest to any inconvenience. Brogan never felt comfortable or safe in a house and managed to find a space in the straw under his horse.

"Just you mind what you're doin'!" he grunted at her as he lay down. She snorted, looked down at him and appeared to have a smile on her face.

As he lay there, Brogan roughly reckoned up how many people had come into the town and he finally reached a total of just over 200. He found it difficult to imagine where that many could have been found since a casual traveller, which he had been, would have had difficulty in finding half a dozen out in the country.

For the most part they had all been much as expected, cowering peons, but there had been something about the last to arrive, some twenty or twenty-five, which had not seemed quite right. It had puzzled him at the time but he had dismissed it as imagination and in any case something which did not concern him. Now, as he lay under his horse listening to others snoring and grunting all about him, he began to wonder. Eventually he smiled and turned over to go to sleep.

★ ★ ★

Brogan was surprised to find that he was the first to rise and he had been forced to do so by a combination of fleas, bugs and ticks. The fleas and bugs rapidly dropped off him but the ticks were firmly attached and bloated with blood. They were a regular hazard and there was only one effective way of dealing with them and that was to burn them off. He found an old cheroot in his saddle-bag and spent ten minutes removing the offensive parasites. By the time he had removed the ticks and wandered into the square, there were other signs of life in the form of various soldiers stumbling out of the houses, yawning and almost without exception giving themselves a good scratch.

Brogan found one of the several

water pumps, worked the handle up and down for a few moments and, when the water suddenly gushed forth, bent down and allowed it to run all over his head. Having satisfied himself that he had washed for the day, he took a mouthful and then sat down to await happenings.

By the time Lieutenant Granta emerged from the house he was using, almost all of the town had woken up and were assembling more out of curiosity than anything else. The lieutenant saw Brogan and called him over.

"It is my custom to take an early morning ride, do you wish to join me, Mr McNally?"

"Is that an invitation or a command?" asked Brogan.

"An invitation," smiled Granta.

"Then I hope you don't mind if I refuse," replied Brogan. "As far as I'm concerned ridin' is strictly a means of gettin' from one point to another."

"As you please," said Granta. "I find

that a good gallop helps to tone me up for the day."

"I wonder if them folk you is about to kill would like to go for a ride?" mused Brogan.

"Perhaps they should have considered the possibility before becoming *bandidos*," said Granta. "You are wasting your time feeling any sorrow for them."

Brogan shrugged. "What time are you goin' to shoot 'em?"

The lieutenant smiled. "I see you are anxious to leave. I do not blame you for that. Strange as it may seem, I shall derive little pleasure in seeing them die, it is such a waste of life but, it was they who chose to do what they did and therefore they must expect not to complain when they must pay the price of their folly. The only exception I make will be seeing Pablo Hemenez die."

While he had been waiting, Brogan's thoughts had drifted back to the last group of peons to arrive and it filled him with a feeling of unease.

"You told me it was a good thing that Hemenez didn't listen to me when I said somethin' was wrong. What would you do if I told you that somethin' was wrong right here?"

The lieutenant looked at him quietly for a few moments and then smiled. "In this case I would say that either your feelings, as good as they may be, are mistaken or that you are simply attempting to worry me."

"And are you worried?"

The lieutenant laughed. "Should I be, Mr McNally?"

"I think so," replied Brogan.

"In what way?"

Brogan thought for a moment and decided that he had said enough and was not prepared to see possibly innocent peons ill-treated in any way.

"Dunno!" he said eventually. "I just got me this feelin', that's all."

Granta too thought for a moment. "Mr McNally, I have great respect for your intuition and I think I would be foolish to ignore you. There is just the possibility that the four men who escaped are planning something. I shall organize a search of the hills around the town."

Brogan almost said that he would be wasting his time but elected to say nothing as he realized that if nothing else he was helping to delay the executions and just possibly give others the opportunity to do something.

As he watched the lieutenant organize his men into four groups and send them off in different directions, Brogan did wonder if he should have said anything. He had half expected Granta to laugh at his suggestion but he realized that he was an ambitious man, a very good soldier and a very cautious one.

Padre Miguel approached Brogan and sat down beside him. "It is rumoured that there are men massing up in the hills ready to attack the soldiers," he said. "I personally have doubts about this and I cannot help but feel that it is brought about by the hand of a certain *gringo* hobo."

Brogan smiled. "Could be!" he conceded. "At least them folk is still alive."

The padre sighed heavily. "*Si*, but for how much longer?"

"Maybe longer'n you think," smiled Brogan.

★ ★ ★

It was midday before the soldiers returned from their fruitless search and Lieutenant Granta rode up to Brogan and shook his head.

"This time your feelings were wrong, Mr McNally," he said. "We have searched everywhere and found nothing. I did not think that any of these spineless peons would have had the nerve to attempt a rescue but, as you see, I leave nothing to chance. Now we must proceed with the business in hand." Padre Miguel was crossing the square and Granta waited for him. "Good-day to you, Padre," he greeted. "Today, once again, you will be a busy man. The executions take place in one hour from now. Please see to it that everyone is assembled in the square."

"It is the kind of business I could well do without, *señor*," replied the padre. "But if it must be so, then I have but one favour to ask of you."

"I shall do my best to grant you that favour," smiled the lieutenant. "What is it?"

"Please do not use the wall of the church as you did before. It is unseemly for the house of God to be used in such a manner."

The lieutenant laughed. "It would seem most appropriate to me, Padre. They will not have so far to go."

"I do not share the joke," said the padre, firmly.

"Possibly it was in bad taste," admitted Granta. "Very well, the executions will take place in the square."

Lieutenant Granta turned his horse and set about the task of organizing his men, leaving Brogan and the padre to deal with and placate various peons with relatives amongst the condemned. Eventually Brogan too wandered off on his own.

"Do not take it too hard," said a voice as Brogan passed by a doorway. He turned to see Anna. She placed a hand on his arm and squeezed gently. "You have done all you can and much more than most."

"Seems my best just wasn't good enough," he said. "Anyhow, no matter what, I'll be on my way as soon as this is all over."

"And you will soon forget that Santa Cruz, Padre Miguel, Lieutenant Granta and I ever existed." She sighed. "Such is the way of things."

"Maybe I will, maybe I won't," said Brogan. "Anyhow, the same goes for you."

"There you are quite wrong," she said softly. "I can never forget you or what you have tried to do."

"Maybe one day you'll be tellin' your grand-kids about this but you won't be able to remember my name. I'll just be some strange Americano who was passin' through."

Further conversation was halted by the arrival of Padre Miguel who was obeying instructions in ordering everyone into the square. Brogan felt a small hand slip into his as he and Anna did what was required of them and joined those already gathered. He made no attempt to dislodge her gentle but firm grip, although he did feel as if everyone else was staring at him. In reality all were far too concerned with what was about to happen to even give Anna and him a second glance.

As everyone gathered, Brogan became aware that the group who arrived last had taken up position directly behind where eight soldiers were lined up. These soldiers were to be the firing squad and for the first time Brogan was able to see the faces of the peons properly. His hand tensed, squeezing Anna's hand quite painfully. She looked up in alarm.

"What is the matter, Señor Brogan?" she whispered. "What is it that you have seen?"

"I ain't sure," Brogan lied. "If I'm right, when the shootin' starts, you just run like hell."

"Shooting?" she queried. "What shooting . . . ?"

"Don't ask damn fool questions," he hissed. "You just do as I say an' get the hell out of it."

"I . . . I do not understand . . . "

"You will," Brogan assured.

9

LIEUTENANT GRANTA rode around the square positioning men to face the crowd and, when he was eventually satisfied, called for the prisoners to be brought out. They shuffled forward, most with heads bowed but a few standing defiantly upright; leading them was Pablo Hemenez, erect and laughing. The soldier alongside him tried to stop his laughter but failed and gave up.

There were twenty-four of them, including Hemenez, and once they were assembled in the square they were split up into three groups, two of eight and one of seven with Hemenez kept to one side. Obviously the *bandido* was going to be executed on his own as some sort of example. After a short pause the first group of eight were led out to the centre of the square and

199

lined up in front of the firing squad.

A heavy silence fell upon the crowd and for a few moments nothing happened and then the lieutenant nodded to a sergeant who barked an order and the men in the firing squad raised their rifles and took aim. All eyes seemed to be on the unfortunate victims, including those of the soldiers around the square . . .

Suddenly there was pandemonium as a volley of shots rang out but it was not the peons who fell, it was the men in the firing squad.

Brogan pushed Anna through the crowd and ordered her to take cover.

He had drawn his Colt but had no intention of using it unless he had to and he too took cover around the corner of a building and watched in fascination the carnage now unfolding.

It seemed that all the men in the firing squad had been shot by the first volley and that a great many other peons were armed as they had suddenly produced guns of all shapes, sizes and age, but at the close range they were to the soldiers, even the ancient scatterguns proved very effective.

Lieutenant Granta had great difficulty in controlling his horse and somehow appeared to have escaped any obvious injury. Gun in hand and still trying to control his horse, he fired at almost anything that moved, but it was only a six-shot revolver and he had soon used all his ammunition and, apparently realizing the hopelessness of the situation, he suddenly turned through a gap in the mob and raced out of town. In the meantime resistance from the soldiers rapidly waned and a few tried to surrender but the peons were in no mood to take prisoners and even Brogan felt slightly sickened at the sight of howling mobs descending upon the soldiers, attacking them with knives and stones.

The whole event was over in a remarkably short time, a matter of two or three minutes at the most, but the mobs were still looking for victims and they managed to find one hiding in a dung heap and they triumphantly dragged him out. Ignoring his pleas for mercy, led him to one of the few trees where a rope was slung over a branch, tied around the soldier's neck and he was jerked off the ground, his feet kicking wildly and his hands trying vainly to loosen the rope. As he struggled someone picked up a stone and hurled it at him. The man's struggles ceased very quickly under a hail of stones. The injured soldier from Mérida was treated much the same.

The peons had not had things entirely their own way, there had been five killed — four men and one woman — and eight or nine injured in one way or another. Two of them looked to be seriously hurt and there were doubts that they would live. However, despite the casualties, nothing could dampen the euphoria of the peons and they danced in the square to the makeshift music of someone who produced a guitar.

Pablo Hemenez and the others had been cut free and he, Hemenez, was busy shaking hands and embracing everyone he came into contact with. Only Padre Miguel, Anna and Brogan did not join in the festivities.

"I fear the worst," sighed Padre Miguel. "Granta has escaped and he will tell the authorities what has happened and they will be bound to send more soldiers. This time they will not hesitate to wipe us all out."

"I reckon so," nodded Brogan. "Don't any of them realize that?"

"I do not think they are in any mood to listen to reason at the moment," said the padre. "I think it will be a long time before reason takes over again."

"You knew this was going to happen," Anna said to Brogan. "How did you know?"

"Somethin' about the way some of them acted last night," said Brogan.

"I didn't see 'em proper then but this mornin' I recognized four of 'em, the men who escaped from Granta at Mérida. There was only one reason they would be here an' it wasn't to watch anyone except the soldiers bein' killed."

"You tried to warn Lieutenant Granta, didn't you?" Anna said again. "That is why he searched the hills this morning."

"I just told him I thought somethin' was wrong," nodded Brogan. "I didn't actually warn him."

"Like the padre," sighed Anna, "I am sure that what has happened is a bad thing. We will all pay for this day."

Pablo Hemenez managed to detach himself from a group of enthusiastic admirers and came over to them. "It is good to see you again, *gringo*," he greeted with a broad grin. "See, my men did not let me down. This is a glorious day, a blow against the authorities. Now they will think twice before taking on Pablo Hemenez."

"You mean they'll send a whole lot more soldiers an' wipe everyone out," said Brogan. "Maybe if you'd killed or caught Lieutenant Granta you might have been in with a chance."

"Let them send the whole of the Mexican Army!" declared Hemenez. "We shall be ready for them and we shall take the revolution through to Mexico City itself."

"I wish you the best of luck," said Brogan. "I still say you might have stood some sort of chance if you'd taken Granta."

"Cautious as ever, *gringo*! I see too that you are not happy, Padre," he said. "It is sad that so many were killed but death is unavoidable in battle."

"It is not for the dead I am sad," replied the padre. "It is for the living. Do you not see that Señor Brogan is right in what he says. Granta will alert the authorities and they will send more soldiers than you could possibly deal with and there will be many more deaths, this time wholly innocent deaths."

Hemenez looked thoughtful. "Perhaps you are right, I do not know. All I know is that at last the people have united and driven out the soldiers. Even if you are right, now is not the moment to tell them. Let them have their moment and the celebrations. With the morning perhaps they will realize."

"And when they do realize," said Anna, "we shall all be forced to leave our homes, our towns and villages. The only chance we may have to survive will be roaming the mountains."

Hemenez shrugged. "It is one way."

"In the meantime there is much work to be done here," said Padre Miguel. "There are many bodies to be buried, we cannot leave them much longer in the heat."

"If'n you don't mind me sayin' so, Padre," said Brogan. "I don't reckon it would be a wise thing to bury the soldiers in town."

"We cannot just leave them!" asserted the padre. "Hated men they may have been in life, but in death all men are equal. They must have a Christian burial."

"That's a matter for you an' the people of Santa Cruz," said Brogan. "All I was thinkin' was that should Lieutenant Granta not make it back for some reason, even if the authorities came searchin', it wouldn't help you if they was to find the bodies of soldiers in your cemetery."

"This time I must agree with you, *gringo*," said Hemenez. "I will admit that it is something my simple brain would never have thought of. No, Padre, we cannot bury the soldiers here, they must be taken out into the hills where the chances of them being found are not very great."

"The Devil's Pit!" Anna suddenly exclaimed. "They will never be found there!"

Padre Miguel looked distinctly uncomfortable. "It is an evil place, it is not wise to go there . . . "

"The perfect place!" exclaimed Hemenez. "She is right, it would be impossible for anyone to find them there."

"I don't want to sound ignorant," said Brogan, "but just what the hell is this Devil's Pit?"

"There is no reason you should know, *gringo*," said Hemenez. "It is a large hole in the ground. The old Indian story is that it was made by the Devil when he drove his stick into the ground. It is very deep and no man has ever been to the bottom, at least none have survived. The sides are sheer and it is impossible to see the bottom."

"Sounds like the perfect place," said Brogan. "The next problem is their horses."

"They should be no trouble," said Hemenez. "Forty horses can be easily lost among the farms or some can be eaten."

"Then I suggest you get the people

on to it as soon as you can an' make sure all evidence that the soldiers have even been here is sent down this pit with the bodies," said Brogan. "Sorry if you don't like it, Padre, but you must see that it makes sense."

Padre Miguel sighed and shook his head. "Perhaps it would be better if we were all dead rather than live a lie."

"You sure will be dead if you don't do somethin'," said Brogan, "you included, but even if you ain't worried for yourself, think of all them kids out there, they haven't done nothin', can you see them die? Anyhow, it'll all mean nothin' if Granta gets back to the authorities."

"Perhaps we should send men after him," suggested Hemenez.

"You could try it," agreed Brogan, "but he's had a hell of a start."

"You are right," grunted Hemenez. "We must hope that some accident happens to him. I will go and order that the bodies of the soldiers be collected and taken to the Devil's Pit."

★ ★ ★

Out of nothing more than idle curiosity, Brogan decided to go with the men taking the bodies. He was very surprised when Padre Miguel and Anna also decided to go. Padre Miguel's reason was that he insisted on giving them the best Christian send-off he could.

Anna's reason was that she thought Brogan would use the moment to ride on without saying goodbye to her. Actually Brogan had intended doing just that.

The Devil's Pit was some seven or eight miles out of town and along what was nothing more than a goat trail and it took almost three hours, slowed up as they were by the horses carrying the bodies, four bodies to each horse and another five horses carrying other things belonging to the army. It was very noticeable to Brogan that neither guns nor ammunition were included amongst these items.

By late afternoon they were over-looking what was indeed a very large, wide, deep hole and even the approach to the rim was very dangerous but there was a narrow trail and ten minutes later Brogan was standing on the edge and peering down.

He thought he could just see water, but he could not be certain. If it was water, then he estimated the depth at more than two thousand feet and smooth and sheer all the way. There was certainly no chance of the bodies being found down there except possibly by buzzards.

With Padre Miguel intoning in Latin, the bodies were unloaded and unceremoniously thrown over the edge. Brogan listened but did not hear any evidence of them reaching the bottom. Pablo Hemenez seemed satisfied and suggested that they started back since it would be dark before they reached Santa Cruz.

"I'll be on my way," said Brogan. "There ain't nothin' more I can do an' I've been around too long anyhow."

"Do you have to go?" whispered Anna, squeezing his arm.

"Yeh, I have to," said Brogan, "I ain't the settlin' type. You'll find yourself a good man soon an' then you can have loads of kids."

"If the soldiers do not return," she said.

Brogan sighed. "Don't see as there's anythin' I can do about that. As much as I'd like to help, I just can't be expected to take on the Mexican Army."

"I do not ask that you should," whispered Anna again. "Perhaps if it is not possible for you to stay then I could go with you."

"No!" growled Brogan, quite alarmed at the prospect. "My kinda life ain't suitable for a woman an' I ain't about to change it."

"He is right, Anna," said Padre Miguel. "Besides, you are needed here.

If we are to have any chance we need women like you."

"To breed children for the soldiers to kill!" she cried. "What kind of life is that? I do not intend having children for . . . "

"This is no life for a *gringo*," said Hemenez, "and the life of a *gringo* woman is not for the likes of you."

She looked at Brogan for a few moments, her eyes filling with tears. "Then go!" she suddenly declared. "Go now before I do something stupid like throw myself into the Devil's Pit . . . " She turned and ran up the slope.

Brogan was tempted to go after her to comfort her but decided against it. He led his horse up the track . . .

★ ★ ★

"*Gringo!*" a voice snarled behind him. Brogan half turned to see the huge *bandido* they called El Torro standing with his rifle aimed at him. "Die, *gringo!*" rasped The Bull, using one of the few words of English he knew. There was nothing Brogan could do . . .

Suddenly a screaming ball of dresses and petticoats hurled itself at The Bull and for a brief moment there was a struggle before the Mexican's foot slipped over the edge and suddenly he disappeared, his cries echoing eerily. Anna had somehow stopped herself from going over the edge and her ashen face looked up at Brogan.

"That was for Manuel, my brother," she panted.

For a few moments their eyes held each other and suddenly he turned and led his horse away as quickly as he could. When he reached firmer ground he briefly looked back and saw Anna still kneeling on the ground, staring at him. He mounted up and urged his old horse forward.

* * *

Although he liked Mexico, Brogan decided that it was time that he was

214

getting back over the border. Normally his forays southward were little more than a distraction, a change of scenery and somewhere a little warmer in the winter months. It was only rarely that something like his experience at Santa Cruz happened but when it did, he always vowed never to venture across the border again. That vow never lasted more than a few months.

Having spent the night high in the hills, he now descended on to an arid plain but crossing such terrain held no fears for him, both he and his horse were used to it and he could usually find something to eat even in the most unlikely spots.

The one thing that had been occupying his thoughts was what was to happen to Santa Cruz. Lieutenant Granta was certain to report what had happened and it was equally certain that soldiers would be sent to exact retribution. As much as he would have liked to have helped, Brogan was very much a realist; there was no way he could keep a whole regiment of soldiers at bay and, reluctantly, he came to the conclusion that the best thing he could do was ride on and forget.

However, it did trouble him that he had refused to allow Anna to accompany him and more than once he was tempted to turn back and take her with him. He might have given it serious thought, but the turn never actually occurred.

★ ★ ★

His thoughts were suddenly interrupted by the sure knowledge that someone was following him, although in the rolling landscape it was impossible to see who or exactly how far behind they were. He was quite certain that whoever it was was following him since a deliberate change of course made no difference. Towards evening he did catch a glimpse of a solitary figure on a horse.

A group of large rocks presented the

ideal opportunity to find out who his shadow was. He pulled up out of sight, hid his horse behind one of the rocks and positioned himself, rifle in hand, atop another. After about fifteen minutes a horse and rider appeared below him.

"Hold it right there!" he commanded. The horse stopped and the rider looked up. "Anna!" gasped Brogan. "What the hell are you doin' out here?"

"It is a free country, or so I keep hearing," she replied. "I have the right to be where I choose."

Brogan grunted and slid off the rock and went over to her. "I guess you got that right," he said. "Why choose to follow me though?"

"I did not know I was following anyone," she pouted.

"That's a lie!" he said. "I changed direction just to see if you would, an' you did."

She looked a little sheepish. "What does it matter if I am following you? Very well, I admit it and now you have found me. What are you going to do with me, send me back to Santa Cruz?"

"I guess I can't do that," he sighed. "Not with what's likely to happen."

"Then you will take me with you?" she smiled.

"Get off that damned horse an' let's talk about this serious like," he said. "It ain't as simple as you think."

"Do you have any water?" she asked. "I have not had a drink since leaving."

"There's a small water-hole back there . . ." He nodded to the rocks. "I'd say the best thing to do would be to spend the night here."

Anna nodded her agreement and dismounted, Brogan taking her horse and leading it to the water-hole and some rough grass that grew around the edges. His own horse had already discovered the water.

He instructed her to gather as much brushwood as she could and anything else that would burn. Eventually he had a fire going and his billy-can full of water and coffee heating up.

"I've got some salt beef an' a few beans," he said, "or if you like I can see what I can catch an' dig up?"

"The only things out here would be lizard or rattlesnake," she grimaced. "I have heard of people eating such things but I have never wanted to try it."

"Good meat," said Brogan. "If you're hungry enough you'll eat anythin'."

"Then I shall eat salt beef," she smiled. "I shall leave delicacies such as lizard and snake for another time."

"Salt beef an' beans it is," grinned Brogan.

★ ★ ★

Brogan had deliberately avoided questioning her until they had eaten and were settled in the cool shade and she too did not seem over-anxious to discuss the matter. Eventually it could not be delayed any longer.

Brogan's mind was made up, there could be no circumstances in which he would agree to Anna staying with him and, rather surprisingly, he discovered that she agreed with him and that all she wanted was for him to help her cross the border. He was concerned as to how she would make her living but decided that she was a big girl and should know her own mind.

Inevitably the subject turned to what would eventually happen to Santa Cruz and both agreed that the future looked extremely bleak for them and it emerged that it had been her mother who had urged her to leave even before they had thrown the bodies of the soldiers into the Devil's Pit.

10

FOR two more days they made their way slowly northward across the desert, during which time Anna was forced to sample the delights of both lizard and snake, seasoned with a few bulbs and roots which Brogan managed to find. She had to admit that neither the lizard nor the snake tasted as bad as she had expected, in fact she said they tasted quite nice. The roots and bulbs she was not quite so certain about.

"Maybe they'll have some decent food," said Brogan pointing towards the horizon. Anna looked hard but could see nothing. "There's some kind of homestead or farm. Whatever it is, they're sure to have some food we can buy even if they don't want to give it to us."

"You have very good eyesight, Señor

Brogan," she smiled. "All I can see is the desert."

"Oh, it's there OK," he laughed. "I guess I've just got used to seein' these things."

It took them almost an hour to reach the rather shabby looking adobe and at first it appeared as if it was deserted but Brogan knew better and opened a door to reveal a man and two small children cowering in the gloom.

"We ain't about to hurt you," said Brogan. "All we want is some food an' water an' possibly somewhere we can bunk for the night." The man looked uncomprehendingly at Brogan and he sighed. "You don't speak English. That's OK, Anna here is Mexican." He called her over and told her to assure the man that they meant no harm.

The man seemed more than relieved to see Anna and to hear his own tongue being spoken and he emerged from the gloom of what was a small shed. Nevertheless, he still gave Brogan a few nervous glances. Anna engaged in an animated conversation with him for some time and Brogan took the opportunity to search the adobe for anything to eat but found very little.

Suddenly Anna was beside him and seemed very excited. "Lieutenant Granta, he is here!" she exclaimed. Brogan looked about and automatically drew his gun. "*Si*, it is true," she continued. "I have seen him. Come, I will show you." She led the way round the back of the building into another small storage cabin.

As his eyes quickly became accustomed to the gloom, Brogan could see a figure clad in military uniform lying on a makeshift bed and a quick examination indicated that he was alive but seemingly unconscious. He nodded to Anna and returned with her to the owner of the adobe, whose name was José Sienna.

"How the Hell did he get here an' what happened? Ask him that," instructed Brogan.

"He has already told me," replied Anna. "It seems that he was out rounding up a few stray goats yesterday when he came across the lieutenant. His horse was dead and he was badly injured. He thinks he was shot."

"There sure is plenty of blood," agreed Brogan. "Maybe we'd better go take another look at him. Where's Josés wife?"

"Dead," said Anna. "She died about a year ago. He has lived here alone with his children ever since, a boy and a girl aged four and two years."

Brogan nodded. "From the mess inside it sure does look like there hasn't been a woman about for a long time an' them kids could be a whole lot cleaner."

Anna laughed derisively. "There speaks a man who claims that soap and water is unnatural!"

"Kids is different," said Brogan, unabashed. "Me, I got a choice, they don't know no better."

"It is their father's business," said

Anna. "Come, let us look at the lieutenant again."

They wafted away the hordes of flies which seemingly almost covered the lieutenant and found his uniform congealed in blood and stuck to various parts of his body. Even from the most cursory of examinations it was plain that he had been shot at least twice, once in his lower leg and once in his shoulder with two more possible wounds in his stomach — it was impossible to tell exactly due to his uniform being stuck to the flesh. It was obvious that the wounds were several days old and must have been inflicted at Santa Cruz.

"We can't leave him here," said Brogan, as he again wafted away the flies which had settled almost as soon as they had flown off. "I'll take him into the house, you go an' clear a space." Anna nodded and Brogan picked up the limp body, receiving a grunt of pain as reward for his effort. By the time he entered the house Anna and José had cleared a space on a rough, plank, bed. The flies were still in evidence but not in such great numbers.

Anna asked José for some rags and some clean water and she cleaned and dressed the wounds as best she could. Besides his leg and shoulder, there was one wound in the lieutenant's side but the bullet appeared to have passed right through.

Brogan had seen enough of wounds of all kinds to have gained a pretty good knowledge of how bad they were and as he examined the leg, which also proved to be broken, he looked up at Anna and shook his head.

"Gangrene!" he declared. "There ain't no way we're goin' to be able to do anythin' about it 'ceptin' maybe take it off."

"If we leave it, he will die," said Anna, quietly. "His shoulder also does not look very good and could turn to gangrene." She studied Brogan's face for a few moments and then nodded.

"I think we are of the same mind. Alive he presents a problem to Santa Cruz, dead it could be that nobody ever discovers what happened."

"It's a thought," agreed Brogan. "But if he's to have any sort of chance that leg has to come off. Have you ever amputated a leg before?"

"A leg, no," she sighed. "I had to remove the arm of my cousin a few months ago after he had it trapped and crushed. It was a terrible experience but a leg should be no more difficult than an arm."

"I ain't actually done it," said Brogan, "but I seen it done a few times."

"But why should we bother?" she asked. "All we have to do is allow him to die."

"Could you do that?" asked Brogan.

Anna did not answer; she walked outside and stood beside José, talking quietly to him. The two children came and clung to her dress and her hands absently caressed them. Eventually she came back into the room and nodded to Brogan.

"Could you just leave him to die?" she asked. "Do not answer that, I think I know. No matter what a man has done to you you would not see him suffer . . . "

"I once shot a man 'cos there was no hope for him," said Brogan. "Kinda like puttin' an injured horse out of its misery."

Anna smiled briefly. "That is different, that was an act of kindness. José tells me that the nearest doctor is more than three days' ride, but that is using a mule, it could be perhaps no more than a day with a horse. However, he swears that this doctor always refuses to leave town and insists that patients are taken to him. It seems he is in great demand by the army and has no need of customers such as José."

"Granta's army," Brogan pointed out.

"Are you prepared to take him?" she asked. "It is the opposite direction you wish to go. Besides, I do not believe that he would survive the journey."

"Neither do I," Brogan agreed. "Have you told José what the problem is?"

"I have not told him the details," she said, "but he knows that it would be bad if Granta was to reach the army."

"And what does he say about it?"

Anna looked at Brogan sharply. "What does it matter what he says, it is none of his business."

"I guess its just as much his business as ours," replied Brogan. "This is his farm an' he did find the lieutenant."

Anna sighed and nodded, her hand reaching down to comfort the child clinging to her dress. She looked down briefly and smiled. "You are quite right, Señor Brogan, These children are very dirty, their hair and clothes need a good wash." With that she scooped up the small girl who laughed for the first time and took her outside where she proceeded to strip off both children and then immerse them in a shallow trough. José produced some soap and a towel and Brogan watched smilingly as the children laughed and giggled as she scrubbed them.

After about half an hour and two very clean children later, Anna sat alongside Brogan as he contemplated a bug scurrying across the earth.

"I have given the matter of Lieutenant Granta much thought," she said. "I have explained a little more to José and he agrees with me. No matter what has happened or might happen, we must do our best to save the life of the lieutenant."

Brogan smiled. "I'm kinda glad you thought that way," he said. "I know it must've been a hard decision, but I don't think you could have lived with it on your mind."

"Could you?" she asked.

Brogan thought for a moment. "Yep!" he said firmly "I might've thought about what I could've done for a few days, but I don't reckon it would've caused me too much lost sleep."

Anna laughed and looked at him almost admiringly. "You are a very strange man, Señor Brogan," she said. "On the one hand you seem to care what happens to those about you and on the other I know that you are ready to end a man's life by one squeeze of the trigger of your gun. How is it that any man can have such opposite personalities?"

Brogan smiled. "Sure, I'll not deny it, I've killed me more'n my share of men an' never turned a hair. The only thing I say is that every one of them men deserved to die; either that or it was a case of me or them, which amounts to the same thing. There's three things I ain't never done; I ain't never murdered a man, I ain't never robbed nobody of anythin' an' I ain't never raped a woman. That's how I am an' I don't intend to be held accountable to anybody for it, which is why I'm a loner an' a drifter. Now, are we goin' to keep on jawin' about me or are we goin' do somethin' about Granta an' his leg?"

★ ★ ★

Lieutenant Granta was stripped, washed and laid out on the only table in the house. Two knives were sharpened and from somewhere in the jumble José produced a meat cleaver. He also found a large needle and some thread. Anna was somewhat dubious about the thread but in the absence of anything better, it had to be used. Water was boiled, the wound cleaned again and the knives and cleaver briefly immersed in the water.

"I am ready," said Anna, gulping nervously and crossing herself. "I only hope that we are doing the right thing."

"If we don't do somethin' he's a dead man for sure," reminded Brogan. "At least even if he dies it won't be because we didn't do our best."

Anna nodded and made the sign of

232

the cross again and picked up the largest knife, held it over Granta's leg and looked appealingly at both Brogan and José and both nodded encouragement. She took a deep breath and cut into the flesh . . .

* * *

"It is done!" Anna sighed, wiping her sweaty forehead. "All we can do now is wait and see what happens."

Brogan had wrapped the severed leg in a rag and had thrown it on the fire, stating that that was the best thing to do with it. José stoked up the fire and coaxed it to burn fiercely, which had the effect of turning an already hot room into something of an inferno. They decided to move the lieutenant outside into some shade and from somewhere José produced a stone jar full of a cooling fruit juice and they sat in silence sipping their drinks for some time, the children taking the opportunity to cling close to Anna.

"Looks like you got yourself a ready-made family," Brogan observed.

Anna blushed and tried to hide her face. "They do not understand what is happening," she said. "Children of this age need a mother."

"Looks to me like they've decided," grinned Brogan.

Anna gave a quick glance at José who was lying back with his eyes closed since he did not speak English and had no idea what was being said.

"I suspect that you are trying to marry me off," she smiled. "I am not sure that I want to be married off just yet."

"I'm just bein' realistic," said Brogan. "It was you who was sayin' that there were no men left in Santa Cruz to marry. Seems to me you could solve two problems."

She laughed, which made José open his eyes and smile at her. "Perhaps I am being difficult," she said. "It was always my intention to marry a man because I loved him, not simply because it was expected of me. You are just like my mother, she would have me marry an idiot if that was all that was available."

Brogan smiled at José and nodded. "Good job he don't understand what the Hell we're talkin' about," he said. "Maybe your mother would have had you marry some decrepit idiot, but he sure ain't decrepit an' he don't strike me as no idiot."

She sighed and squeezed the little girl who had now clambered on to her lap. "I think that he is a good, hard-working man and I believe he would make a fine and loyal husband, but I do not know him. I know you are right in what you say but I am unsure. I must think about it. Besides, neither you nor I know if he wants to marry me and I am certainly not going to ask him; it is for the man to ask the woman."

Brogan looked at José who once again resumed his almost horizontal position and closed his eyes. "He will," he pronounced with certainty. "Anyhow, you got plenty of time to get to know him, you ain't got no place to go."

She looked at Brogan long and hard for some time before suddenly placing the girl on the ground and standing up. "You are right about this place needing a woman's touch," she sighed. She took the girl's hand and led her into the house. "If you two do not mind, we have women's work to do."

★ ★ ★

Lieutenant Granta blinked and stared up at the face leaning over him, blinked again and tried to sit up. The effort proved too much and he sank back again, sighing and wincing.

"You've had a close run," said Brogan. "Take it easy."

"Mr McNally, it is you," said the lieutenant. "I thought perhaps that I was either dreaming or I had arrived in Hell to find you there before me. Perhaps this is Hell."

"It sure ain't no Heaven," grinned Brogan, "an' it could be Hell for all I know. Only thing is I don't think any of us is dead, leastways if we are it don't feel no different to bein' alive."

The lieutenant struggled to lean on his elbow and looked down at the rough blanket covering the lower half of his body. "Something is wrong," he said. "I am not sure what it is, but I know something is wrong."

"Could be 'cos you now have one leg less than you had a couple of days ago," grinned Brogan.

Granta looked most alarmed and stared in disbelief for a moment before suddenly throwing back the blanket and then raising the bandaged stump. He oathed in Spanish and sank back and stared up in silence at the roof for a few minutes. Eventually he raised the stump again and stared at it.

"Now I know I am in Hell," he said hoarsely. "Where am I?"

"Out in the middle of nowhere," said Brogan. "So I guess you could be right about it bein' Hell. You was found by José — he owns this place — an' me an' Anna came along. That was pure chance, we didn't know which way you'd gone after you rode out of Santa Cruz."

"Anna!" said Granta. "The last thing I remember clearly was gunfire." He suddenly sat up and grimaced with pain. "My men, what happened to my men?"

"What men?" asked Anna as she came through the door. "We know nothing about any men."

"The shooting!" insisted Granta. "You were there, you must know what I am talking about."

"We know nothing of any shooting," said Anna. "Now, lie down while I see to your shoulder, it needs much attention if we are to prevent gangrene. You have a couple of smaller wounds but they are healing well."

"Do not play games with me!" roared the lieutenant. "I am no fool, I know what happened."

"And you know we had to remove your leg," said Anna, forcing him to lie back, "and if you do not allow me to see to your shoulder you may lose your arm too!"

He sighed heavily and allowed her to remove the bandage and clean his shoulder but when she had finished and left, he pulled himself up and stared at Brogan.

"If you think you can buy my silence, Mr McNally, you are quite wrong. I now remember what happened in Santa Cruz and it is my duty to report it to my superiors."

"I guess you've got to do what you think is right," said Brogan. "Me, I didn't have nothin' to do with anythin' that happened, in fact I seem to remember warnin' you that somethin' was wrong."

Granta smiled weakly and nodded. "*Touché* once again, Mr McNally. You did indeed warn me and I took your warning seriously and searched the area but found nothing."

"Just goes to prove you should've searched closer to home," said Brogan. "Anyhow, the thought of buyin' your silence never entered either my or Anna's head. Like I say, you was found out in the desert underneath a dead horse. José brought you here an' then me an' Anna came along. It was Anna who took your leg off, it was pretty badly smashed and completely rotten."

Granta lay back again and stared at the roof for a moment. "I find it strange that either of you should do such a thing. I think that all my men were killed. They cannot get away with it, I shall inform my superiors and the bodies will be discovered and who knows what will happen."

"I wouldn't place too much store on the bodies bein' found," said Brogan. "No bodies, no proof 'ceptin' your word."

"And my word will be sufficient," assured Granta. "You were both very foolish to do what you did. It would have been more logical to have left me in the desert to die."

"Logic is a word I don't understand the meanin' of," laughed Brogan. "Ask my horse, she's tried to make me be logical more'n once. Anyhow, you're alive an' I guess you'll just have to do what you think is right. I'll be around for a day or two if you want to talk."

★ ★ ★

Two days later Lieutenant Granta managed, with the aid of a makeshift crutch fashioned from a branch, to hobble outside and join Brogan and Anna.

"My shoulder, it is not good," he complained. "I must get to a doctor quickly."

"Just head due south for about three days an' you might find one," said Brogan.

"I meant for you to take me to one," said Granta.

"No chance!" smiled Brogan. "I done

my bit, the rest is up to you." The lieutenant looked at Anna questioningly who also shook her head. "Seems like you is on your own," continued Brogan. "It's a hell of a long walk, maybe it'll take you more'n three days, probably will. Your horse is dead an' there ain't no spare horses here."

"I would never make it and you know it," said Granta. "Very well, Mr McNally, you have my word that neither you nor Anna will be implicated in what happened at Santa Cruz."

"What did happen?" mused Brogan. "I ain't too clear about it an' since you ran out I don't see as how you can know what happened."

"Playing word games with me will do you no good," grunted the lieutenant. "I would imagine that I am more adept than you at such games, as clever as you may be."

Brogan smiled, suspecting that Granta might well be right. "Very well," he said, "no word games. Personally I don't see what the hell I can do about it an' it sure as hell won't bother me too much. I'll just carry on like I did before, which is more'n can be said for you."

"Which means what, exactly?"

"He means that whatever happens," said Anna, "whatever you do or say, your time as a soldier has ended. Your shoulder is getting worse, you must know that, and even if you do not lose your arm, a one-legged man is of little use to the army." She seemed almost elated at the thought.

The lieutenant looked at them both thoughtfully for a few moments and then glanced down at his leg. It seemed that her words had reinforced that which he had already thought about and he was none too pleased at the prospect.

"I know nothing else," he said quietly. "Unfortunately you are quite right. The best I could hope for would be some administrative post and I would find that unacceptable." He lapsed into another long silence

243

and eventually sighed and looked up at them. "There is something else which I do not think you have considered, but then why should you?"

"You mean they will blame you for what happened?" asked Brogan.

Granta smiled and nodded. "I see that I have underestimated your abilities, Mr McNally. Yes, I fear that I shall be arrested and have to face a military court. They do not take very kindly to any officer who loses an entire troop. The occasional casualty is accepted as normal, one of the hazards, but it would be impossible for them to accept that I lost over forty men. More to the point, the fact that I deserted them, no matter what the circumstances, is alone sufficient to ensure my disgrace and probable execution."

"Seems like you got a problem," smiled Brogan.

"Indeed I do have a problem," sighed Granta. "And yet I feel duty-bound to report what happened. Be sure that retribution on Santa Cruz will be swift and brutal but it will not save me."

"Then when you've found your doctor, just keep on ridin'," suggested Brogan.

"I am a soldier, for the moment at least," said Granta. "As such, any doctor who treats me has to report the fact to the authorities."

"Then just keep on goin'," said Brogan.

★ ★ ★

Another day passed and the lieutenant's shoulder was getting worse and all knew that it would not be too long before gangrene set in, if it had not done so already. Brogan had been asking questions and had discovered that the border was about two days' ride away and that there was a small town just across the border and that José thought they had a doctor. It was the lieutenant's only chance and he put the proposition to him.

It did not take the lieutenant very

long to make up his mind, although he did stress that he might still feel it his duty to report what had happened at Santa Cruz.

During the preceding twenty-four hours, it had become obvious that Anna had more or less made up her mind about José. She had spent almost all her time cleaning up and reorganizing things, even instructing José to make some more furniture. Brogan managed to catch her between jobs and explained what he was about to do.

"It is what you must do," she sighed. "For myself, I have decided that I can go no further. José has asked me to stay with him and to marry him as soon as we can get to a priest." She smiled a little self-consciously. "You were right, he is a good man and I have accepted him."

"Glad to hear it," said Brogan. "Everythin' will be all right, you'll see."

"I hope so," she smiled. "I was worrying about my mother in Santa

Cruz. As much as I love her, I could not live with her although José did suggest that I bring her here."

"I suspect that he hoped you'd refuse," grinned Brogan.

Anna leaned towards him and suddenly threw her arm round his neck and kissed his cheek. "Thank you," she whispered, "thank you for everything you have done." She released his neck and clasped his hand. "When do you leave?"

"No time like the present," smiled Brogan. "I was hopin' you'd let us have your horse; after all it's obviously an army horse, it's even got an army brand an' anyone snoopin' round might ask a few difficult questions."

"Take it," she smiled. "We have two mules and mules are much more suitable in this land. Just give me time to prepare some food for your journey."

"You got half an hour," grinned Brogan. "It'll take me that long to saddle up an' get the lieutenant aboard."

★ ★ ★

It was shortly before midday when Brogan and the lieutenant started out, which was just about the worst time of day since the sun was at its height and hottest. However, Brogan and his horse had travelled in such conditions many times and were used to it, but it rapidly became obvious that Lieutenant Granta was suffering in the heat. After less than an hour Brogan was forced to call a halt in the shade of some rocks and a small, muddy pool. The lieutenant spent almost the whole of the next two hours sleeping but seemed more able and ready to continue as the heat of the sun began to wane. They rode for another two hours, when they came to a river and decided that it was about the best place to spend the night. However, Brogan was uneasy. For at least half an hour he had been quite convinced that they were being followed and as soon as he had seen that the lieutenant was settled — his shoulder was becoming redder and more puffy — he disappeared among what few tress and scrub grew along the river.

★ ★ ★

"The *gringo*!" A gun suddenly jammed hard into the lieutenant's head. "Where is the *gringo*?" demanded the harsh voice.

Lieutenant Granta looked up into the cruel features glaring at him. "Hemenez!" he croaked.

"*Si*," grated the *bandido*. "I have been searching for you. I saw you riding with someone and I think that someone was the *gringo*, McNally."

"Thought it was you," rasped Brogan from behind. "You never learn, I can almost smell folk like you from ten miles."

Pablo Hemenez did not move but he laughed, keeping his gun firmly at the lieutenant's head. "It is good to see you again, *gringo*," he laughed. "I

249

came across Anna shortly after you left her and she told me which direction you had gone and who with. I am puzzled, *gringo*. I am puzzled that you should help a man such as Granta."

"I'd do the same for you," said Brogan.

"*Si*," grinned Hemenez, "I believe that you would. However, I do not have the same honour which you have. I have found the one I came looking for and I intend to kill him. It is no longer any of your business, *gringo*, you are free to go."

"Go ahead an' shoot," invited Brogan. "It ain't often I shoot a man in the back, but I've done it before when it's been necessary an' I ain't afraid to do it again."

"You would kill me to save a man who you know would say things which would lead to even more deaths?" said Hemenez. "Is that honour? Is it not better to exterminate one man than know that if you do not that many many others will surely die?"

"I'm takin' him over the border," said Brogan.

"And as an officer in the Mexican Army he will be sent back straight away," said Hemenez.

"That ain't my problem," said Brogan.

"But it is mine," snarled Hemenez. "Granta is vermin to my people and I exterminate all vermin. I do not think you will shoot me, *gringo*."

"Just try me!" invited Brogan.

Hemenez glanced behind him and saw Brogan with his gun aimed steadily at him. He smiled and nodded briefly "I do believe that you would do it." He eased back the hammer on his gun and slipped it into the belt around his chest and shoulder. "Very well, for the moment you win but remember that I am only a rifle shot away and I am a very good shot. It could be that I will have to kill you both so where does that leave you? You now have the upper hand, but for how long? Are you prepared to kill someone in cold blood just to protect a man like Granta?"

251

"Just remember I got eyes up my arse," hissed Brogan. "I knew you were behind me."

Hemenez smiled and nodded. "*Si*, I know that I could never surprise you. But there will be many opportunities between here and the border."

"On your horse," instructed Brogan. "An' just thank God that I didn't shoot you."

Hemenez laughed. "It is there that you and I differ. You cannot kill an unarmed man. Is it not your boast that you have never committed a murder? Me, I could put a bullet through his head and not even think about it."

"Not while I'm holdin' this gun," said Brogan.

"*Si*," grinned Hemenez, strolling to where he had tethered his horse. "How long will you be holding your gun, *gringo*?" He laughed coarsely.

The *bandido* led his horse from behind some brush and for a brief moment the animal was between him and Brogan. There was a sudden cry from the lieutenant, followed by a shot which singed Brogan's cheek.

Brogan reacted quickly and was rolling along the ground firing at Hemenez and two shots thudded into the *bandido*, but that did not prevent him from firing another shot at Lieutenant Granta and from the way his body arched, Brogan knew that it had found its mark with deadly accuracy. Hemenez slid to the ground, dropping his gun and Brogan ran to the lieutenant to find blood oozing from his chest into his dirty uniform. He was still alive but instinctively Brogan knew he had not long. He had drawn his gun and now clutched it as he grinned up at Brogan.

"You have solved two problems," rasped Granta. "Now nobody need ever know what happened at Santa Cruz. Please, before I die, what did happen to the bodies of my men?"

"Down some place called the Devil's Pit," said Brogan.

"Ah, *si*, I should have guessed."

He looked past Brogan. "Please, Mr McNally, move to one side." Brogan instinctively did so and looked behind him. A single shot rang out close to his ear and Pablo Hemenez, who had managed to struggle to his knees and find his gun, gasped and collapsed. "At least I have killed the man I was instructed to kill," rasped Granta. He gave a choked gasp and closed his eyes.

Both men were dead and Brogan did what he usually did and left the bodies where they were as food for the buzzards and coyotes. The horses he took in tow the next day and deposited with a rather bewildered looking Mexican homesteader and without saying a word, continued to the border.

Other titles in the Linford Western Library:

TOP HAND
Wade Everett

The Broken T was big. But no ranch is big enough to let a man hide from himself.

GUN WOLVES OF LOBO BASIN
Lee Floren

The Feud was a blood debt. When Smoke Talbot found the outlaws who gunned down his folks he aimed to nail their hide to the barn door.

SHOTGUN SHARKEY
Marshall Grover

The westbound coach carrying the indomitable Larry and Stretch headed for a shooting showdown.

FIGHTING RAMROD
Charles N. Heckelmann

Most men would have cut their losses, but Frazer counted the bullets in his guns and said he'd soak the range in blood before he'd give up another inch of what was his.

LONE GUN
Eric Allen

Smoke Blackbird had been away too long. The Lequires had seized the Blackbird farm, forcing the Indians and settlers off, and no one seemed willing to fight! He had to fight alone.

THE THIRD RIDER
Barry Cord

Mel Rawlins wasn't going to let anything stand in his way. His father was murdered, his two brothers gone. Now Mel rode for vengeance.

ARIZONA DRIFTERS
W. C. Tuttle

When drifting Dutton and Lonnie Steelman decide to become partners they find that they have a common enemy in the formidable Thurston brothers.

TOMBSTONE
Matt Braun

Wells Fargo paid Luke Starbuck to outgun the silver-thieving stagecoach gang at Tombstone. Before long Luke can see the only thing bearing fruit in this eldorado will be the gallows tree.

HIGH BORDER RIDERS
Lee Floren

Buckshot McKee and Tortilla Joe cut the trail of a border tough who was running Mexican beef into Texas. They stopped the smuggler in his tracks.

BRETT RANDALL, GAMBLER
E. B. Mann

Larry Day had the choice of running away from the law or of assuming a dead man's place. No matter what he decided he was bound to end up dead.

THE GUNSHARP
William R. Cox

The Eggerleys weren't very smart. They trained their sights on Will Carney and Arizona's biggest blood bath began.

THE DEPUTY OF SAN RIANO
Lawrence A. Keating and
Al. P. Nelson

When a man fell dead from his horse, Ed Grant was spotted riding away from the scene. The deputy sheriff rode out after him and came up against everything from gunfire to dynamite.

FARGO: MASSACRE RIVER
John Benteen

The ambushers up ahead had now blocked the road. Fargo's convoy was a jumble, a perfect target for the insurgents' weapons!

SUNDANCE: DEATH IN THE LAVA
John Benteen

The Modoc's captured the wagon train and its cargo of gold. But now the halfbreed they called Sundance was going after it . . .

HARSH RECKONING
Phil Ketchum

Five years of keeping himself alive in a brutal prison had made Brand tough and careless about who he gunned down . . .

FARGO: PANAMA GOLD
John Benteen

With foreign money behind him, Buckner was going to destroy the Panama Canal before it could be completed. Fargo's job was to stop Buckner.

FARGO: THE SHARPSHOOTERS
John Benteen

The Canfield clan, thirty strong were raising hell in Texas. Fargo was tough enough to hold his own against the whole clan.

PISTOL LAW
Paul Evan Lehman

Lance Jones came back to Mustang for just one thing — revenge! Revenge on the people who had him thrown in jail.

HELL RIDERS
Steve Mensing

Wade Walker's kid brother, Duane, was locked up in the Silver City jail facing a rope at dawn. Wade was a ruthless outlaw, but he was smart, and he had vowed to have his brother out of jail before morning!

DESERT OF THE DAMNED
Nelson Nye

The law was after him for the murder of a marshal — a murder he didn't commit. Breen was after him for revenge — and Breen wouldn't stop at anything . . . blackmail, a frameup . . . or murder.

DAY OF THE COMANCHEROS
Steven C. Lawrence

Their very name struck terror into men's hearts — the Comancheros, a savage army of cutthroats who swept across Texas, leaving behind a bloodstained trail of robbery and murder.

SUNDANCE: SILENT ENEMY
John Benteen

A lone crazed Cheyenne was on a personal war path. They needed to pit one man against one crazed Indian. That man was Sundance.

LASSITER
Jack Slade

Lassiter wasn't the kind of man to listen to reason. Cross him once and he'll hold a grudge for years to come — if he let you live that long.

LAST STAGE TO GOMORRAH
Barry Cord

Jeff Carter, tough ex-riverboat gambler, now had himself a horse ranch that kept him free from gunfights and card games. Until Sturvesant of Wells Fargo showed up.

McALLISTER ON THE COMANCHE CROSSING
Matt Chisholm

The Comanche, McAllister owes them a life — and the trail is soaked with the blood of the men who had tried to outrun them before.

QUICK-TRIGGER COUNTRY
Clem Colt

Turkey Red hooked up with Curly Bill Graham's outlaw crew. But wholesale murder was out of Turk's line, so when range war flared he bucked the whole border gang alone . . .

CAMPAIGNING
Jim Miller

Ambushed on the Santa Fe trail, Sean Callahan is saved by two Indian strangers. But there'll be more lead and arrows flying before the band join Kit Carson against the Comanches.

GUNSLINGER'S RANGE
Jackson Cole

Three escaped convicts are out for revenge. They won't rest until they put a bullet through the head of the dirty snake who locked them behind bars.

RUSTLER'S TRAIL
Lee Floren

Jim Carlin knew he would have to stand up and fight because he had staked his claim right in the middle of Big Ike Outland's best grass.

THE TRUTH ABOUT SNAKE RIDGE
Marshall Grover

The troubleshooters came to San Cristobal to help the needy. For Larry and Stretch the turmoil began with a brawl and then an ambush.

WOLF DOG RANGE
Lee Floren

Will Ardery would stop at nothing, unless something stopped him first — like a bullet from Pete Manly's gun.

DEVIL'S DINERO
Marshall Grover

Plagued by remorse, a rich old reprobate hired the Texas Trouble-shooters to deliver a fortune in greenbacks to each of his victims.

GUNS OF FURY
Ernest Haycox

Dane Starr, alias Dan Smith, wanted to close the door on his past and hang up his guns, but people wouldn't let him.

DONOVAN
Elmer Kelton

Donovan was supposed to be dead. Uncle Joe Vickers had fired off both barrels of a shotgun into the vicious outlaw's face as he was escaping from jail. Now Uncle Joe had been shot — in just the same way.

CODE OF THE GUN
Gordon D. Shirreffs

MacLean came riding home, with saddle tramp written all over him, but sewn in his shirt-lining was an Arizona Ranger's star.

GAMBLER'S GUN LUCK
Brett Austen

Gamblers seldom live long. Parker was a hell of a gambler. It was his life — or his death . . .